"*You belong to me.*"

Mary Beth felt the steam rising in her and opened her mouth to blast him with it when he quickly held up his arms in a defensive gesture. "Sorry. I apologize," he said hastily. "I knew that was the wrong thing to say the second it was out. You don't belong to me. Intellectually I know that, but..."

He put down his arms and again took her hand. "When we said our marriage vows I agreed to love and cherish you, to care for you in sickness and in health until death parted us. I took that vow seriously. I cherished you, took care of you—"

"But you didn't love me." The words had a strangled sound as tears welled in her blue eyes.

"I did love you," he said desperately as his hand tightened on hers.

Dear Reader:

Happy holidays! Our authors join me in wishing you all the best for a joyful, loving holiday season with your family and friends. And while celebrating the new year—and the new decade!—I hope you'll think of Silhouette Books.

1990 promises to be especially happy here. This year marks our tenth anniversary, and we're planning a celebration! To symbolize the timelessness of love, as well as the modern gift of the tenth anniversary, each month in 1990, we're presenting readers with a *Diamond Jubilee* Silhouette Romance title, penned by one of your all-time favorite Silhouette Romance authors.

In January, under the Silhouette Romance line's *Diamond Jubilee* emblem, look for Diana Palmer's next book in her bestselling LONG, TALL TEXANS series—*Ethan*. He's a hero sure to lasso your heart! And just in time for Valentine's Day, Brittany Young has written *The Ambassador's Daughter*. Spend the most romantic month of the year in France, the setting for this magical classic. Victoria Glenn, Annette Broadrick, Peggy Webb, Dixie Browning, Phyllis Halldorson—to name just a few!—have written *Diamond Jubilee* titles especially for you. And Pepper Adams has penned a trilogy about three very rugged heroes—and their lovely heroines!—set on the plains of Oklahoma. Look for the first book this summer.

The *Diamond Jubilee* celebration is Silhouette Romance's way of saying thanks to you, our readers. We've been together for ten years now, and with the support you've given us, you can look forward to many more years of heartwarming, poignant love stories.

I hope you'll enjoy this book and all of the stories to come. Come home to romance—Silhouette Romance—for always!

Sincerely,

Tara Hughes Gavin
Senior Editor

PHYLLIS HALLDORSON

Dream Again of Love

Silhouette Romance

Published by Silhouette Books New York

America's Publisher of Contemporary Romance

SILHOUETTE BOOKS
300 E. 42nd St., New York, N.Y. 10017

ISBN: 0-373-08689-X

First Silhouette Books printing December 1989

All the characters in this book are fictitious. Any
resemblance to actual persons, living or dead, is
purely coincidental.

Printed in the U.S.A.

Books by Phyllis Halldorson

Silhouette Romance

Temporary Bride #31
To Start Again #79
Mountain Melody #247
If Ever I Loved Again #282
Design for Two Hearts #367
Forgotten Love #395
An Honest Lover #456
To Choose a Wife #515
Return to Raindance #566
Raindance Autumn #584
Ageless Passion, Timeless Love #653
Dream Again of Love #689

Silhouette Special Edition

My Heart's Undoing #290
The Showgirl and the Professor #368
Cross My Heart #430
Ask Not of Me, Love #510

PHYLLIS HALLDORSON

At age sixteen Phyllis Halldorson met her real-life Prince Charming. She married him a year later, and they settled down to raise a family. A compulsive reader, Phyllis dreamed of someday finding the time to write stories of her own. That time came when her two youngest children reached adolescence. When she was introduced to romance novels, she knew she had found her long-delayed vocation. After all, how could she write anything else after living all those years with her very own Silhouette hero?

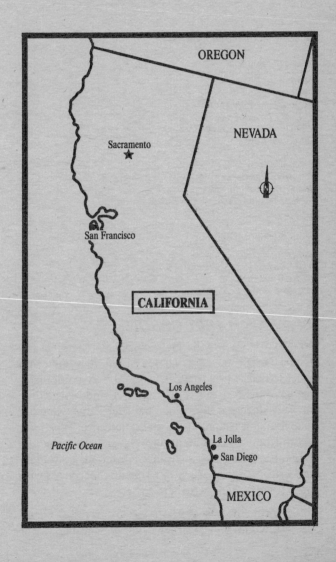

Chapter One

Mary Elizabeth Warren was aware that she was dreaming. It was the same dream that had tormented her for years, only this time it was as if there were two of her, one standing aside and watching, while the other played out her role in the all-too-familiar scene.

Mary Beth watched herself as she drove up to the impressive brick Tudor-style house in the red Jaguar Flynn had bought her for her twenty-first birthday six months before.

The Mary Beth in the dream was excited and happy. She'd been away, but had come home early to surprise Flynn. It was late at night, and she quietly let herself in. The lights were on in the foyer and the living room, but the rooms were empty. She seemed to float as she went looking for her husband.

Then she saw a light under the closed door of Flynn's den. How like him to bring paperwork home after he'd already spent a full day at the hospital. Well, she had better ways to occupy his time for the rest of the night.

The Mary Beth that watched knew what was coming and struggled desperately to wake up. The dream slowed when the other Mary Beth, eager to be in her husband's arms again, put her hand on the doorknob and turned it.

The scene that greeted her inside the den never varied from its real-life counterpart. Shock and heartbreak shattered her again as she stared at Flynn, the husband she adored, and Vanessa, his ex-fiancée from long ago, locked in an embrace. He'd apparently heard the door open and looked up, but Vanessa's face was still lifted to his, her arms holding him close, and his expression was a startled mixture of shock and unmistakable guilt.

When she finally wrenched herself out of the dream, Mary Beth was sitting bolt upright in the middle of her bed in total darkness, trembling and with tears streaming down her cheeks. The staggering blow she'd sustained at that moment rocked her again, and she drew up her knees and buried her face in them as she wrapped her arms around her legs and let the silent sobs shake her.

Awake, she no longer cried for her broken marriage; she cried because after three years the dream still came back to haunt her. It had been months since its last appearance, and she'd convinced herself that she'd finally banished it for good.

Why had it come back now? She hadn't even thought about Flynn in weeks. Was he merely hiding in her subconscious, waiting to pounce when all her defenses were down?

Darn him! He hadn't wanted her. She'd given him his freedom. Why did he still come back to haunt her dreams?

She reached over and turned on the bedside lamp. It was only a little past four in the morning, but she was too worked up to go back to sleep.

Without bothering to put a robe over her pink brushed-satin nightgown or run a comb through the light blond hair that spilled over her shoulders, she crept quietly down the hall toward the kitchen. She didn't want to waken her apartment mate and fellow teacher, Peggy MacGregor, but she needed a cup of hot coffee.

The light from her bedroom didn't extend to the two front rooms, and Mary Beth felt her way through the dark living room and into the kitchen, where she found the light switch and flipped it. The bright, cheerful yellow room was large but it did double duty as a dining room, and the formal oak table and six chairs stood at one end.

She had prepared the coffee maker and turned it on when a male voice, gravelly with sleep, spoke from behind her. "What are you doing up at this ungodly hour?"

Her blood ran cold. Flynn?

My God, her dream had seemed real, but... With a cry of disbelief she spun around to see the figure of a man clad only in a pair of jeans, standing just out of the light in the doorway. Before she could react, he stepped into the light and she saw that it was neither an apparition of her ex-husband nor a burglar. It was Donald MacGregor, Peggy's brother. She'd been dating him on a fairly regular basis.

She'd forgotten that he was spending the night on their sofa while the fresh paint in his own apartment dried.

"Oh, Don." Her voice was little more than a whisper, and she clutched the counter with one hand to steady herself as the room seemed to spin.

Don bounded across the kitchen and took her in his arms. "Mary Beth, what's the matter? Are you sick?"

The embrace, tender and concerned, but so unlike Flynn's hard passion, restored her equilibrium and she leaned into it. Don was tall, six feet two inches, and bony. She'd never encountered his bare flesh before, and it was smooth and muscular, unlike Flynn's firm hard physique with the mat of light brown curls covering his chest and narrowing down his flat belly.

Without warning, the tears she'd so recently conquered came flooding back, and she sobbed against his chest.

He held her close and murmured into her hair, "Honey, it's all right. Tell me what's wrong. Did I scare you?"

"I'm sorry," she said as she struggled for control. "I had a bad dream and couldn't go back to sleep. I'd forgotten you were here, and when you spoke..." Her voice broke, and she gave up and just let him hold her.

Why couldn't she fall in love with Don? He was nice and understanding and industrious. At age twenty-six he was an electrical engineer with a good job at the San Diego division of General Dynamics and had excellent prospects. He'd indicated a more than casual interest in her, but it wouldn't be fair for her to encourage him when she knew she'd never be able to respond to him in the way a wife or lover should.

They were standing there wrapped in each other's arms when there was a gasp from the doorway. They both turned to confront a tall, angular, auburn-haired woman with high cheekbones, a wide mouth and the stance and beauty of a fashion model.

It was Peggy wearing a terry cloth robe, her green eyes reflecting her surprise. "Oh, sorry," she said, her tone laced with embarrassment as she turned to leave.

"No, wait," Mary Beth and Don called in unison.

"Hey, sis, it's no big deal," Don continued as Peggy turned toward them again. "If I'd intended to seduce Mary Beth, I'd have had enough class to arrange for a hotel room. The floor of the kitchen just isn't my style." His eyes danced with amusement.

Peggy looked abashed. "Then I suggest you both put some clothes on."

Mary Beth's face burned as she looked at Don and then down at herself. He was nude except for a hastily donned pair of jeans, and although she was covered from chin to ankles, her shimmering satin-and-lace gown was definitely seductive. No doubt her tousled hair didn't help her image, either.

She had to admit that they looked like lovers caught after a night of unbridled passion!

Knowing her face was flaming, she took a deep breath and hurried to speak. "Come on in, Peggy. I had a bad dream and came out to make a pot of coffee. Sit down and have a cup while Don and I get dressed. Then I'll explain everything."

Ten minutes later Mary Beth had changed into jeans and a sweatshirt, and Don had put on his shirt and shoes. They were sitting at the table with Peggy, and Mary Beth had just finished explaining why she and Don were embracing in the kitchen before dawn on this early September morning.

Peggy was the first to respond. "Do you want to talk about this recurring dream that upsets you so? I don't mean to pry, but sometimes it helps to discuss it with someone."

The idea appealed to Mary Beth. There'd never been anyone she could discuss the dream with. In the beginning she hadn't wanted to burden Flynn's family, who were already upset over the breakup of the marriage, and later, when she'd lived in Spain, she'd felt the subject was too deeply personal to expose to her new friends.

She ran her fingers through her long hair in an effort to keep it away from her face. "If you're sure you don't mind listening, I think it might help to share it with the two of you."

Both Don and Peggy assured her that since it was Saturday and neither of them had to go to work, they had plenty of time to hear anything she wanted to tell them.

She hesitated a moment, wondering where to begin. "I guess I'm going to have to start at the beginning of my life in order to make you understand everything," she finally said.

Don chuckled. "I doubt if you've managed to pack so much living into just twenty-four years that it'll take all that long in the telling."

Her mouth turned up in a sad little smile. "Actually, that's exactly what I've done. My parents were teaching missionaries in Central America. I lived there from the time I was four until I was seventeen."

"Mary Beth, I knew you'd grown up there, but you never talk about it." Peggy sounded anything but bored. "What are their school systems like down there?"

Since she and Mary Beth were both elementary school teachers, that was a natural question.

"I never attended the public schools. I was taught at the mission along with the native children. We were in an isolated, underdeveloped area where the only school was the one the missionaries taught."

Peggy frowned. "But weren't you lonesome?"

"Not at all. I grew up with the native children. I spoke Spanish as easily as I spoke English, and I was very happy. I didn't even realize how appallingly primitive the living conditions were because I had nothing to compare them to.''

"Weren't you in danger?" Don asked. "The political climate in those countries is always precarious."

She nodded. "Yes, we were, but I didn't realize that until..." Her voice broke, and she tried again. "Until shortly before I left."

Don swore. "What were your parents thinking of, taking a child into a situation like that?"

She was surprised at her defensive reaction even after all those years. She resented the implied criticism of her beloved mother and father. "You have to understand that my parents were very special people. They loved me. I never doubted that, but they also had great compassion for the underprivileged children of the world. They devoted their lives to educating those children, and I'm a much better person for having had the privilege of being raised by them. Even though there was a certain amount of danger and discomfort involved."

Don looked stricken. "Oh, hey, I'm sorry. I didn't mean...that is..."

She took pity on him and patted his hand where it lay on the table. "I know. It's okay. I'm sorry, it's just that—"

"Are they still in the missionary field?" Peggy asked in an obvious effort to change the subject.

The old pain of loss and loneliness stole over her as she shook her head. "No. I'll explain later."

She cleared her throat. "To get on, when I was sixteen, a medical clinic was established nearby, and one of the staff doctors was a young American, Flynn Warren, who had just completed his residency in pediatrics and was serving a two-year stint as a medical missionary."

She closed her eyes and could see him as clearly as if he were standing before her. "I'd had little contact with Anglo men except for the middle-aged and elderly missionaries who came and went, and Flynn was the most beautiful male I'd ever seen. He was tall and slender with light brown hair and eyes."

And his mouth. Oh, God, the mouth that could make her shiver with happiness when it turned up, and plunge her into despair when it turned down. The lips that introduced her to ecstasy, and in the end betrayed her.

"So what happened?" Peggy asked impatiently, and Mary Beth's eyes flew open as she realized she'd been daydreaming.

"Oh, I...I'm afraid I was smitten right from the beginning. I'd never had a boy-girl relationship with any of the native boys. They were friends, but neither my parents nor theirs would have approved of even the most innocent romance. It had always been understood that when I could qualify, I would be sent back to this country for a college education."

Don grinned. "You expect me to believe that you managed to reach the age of sweet sixteen without ever being kissed?"

She grinned back. "I'm afraid that's the way it was. Anyway, it's not surprising that I was practically struck dumb by a man like Flynn Warren. All the adolescent crushes I should have had came together and focused on him.

"I was painfully shy and unworldly, and although I didn't realize it at the time, my feelings were transparent. Both Flynn and my parents were aware of them, but Flynn, not wanting to hurt or embarrass me, treated me in the same friendly, relaxed manner as he did the adults.

He was careful, though, to mention Vanessa, the fiancée who was waiting for him back home in Baltimore."

She stopped for a moment and drank the rest of her cooling coffee. What a lovesick child she'd been.

"I was well aware that vows, both betrothal and nuptial between a man and a woman, were sacred," she explained, "and I never flirted with him or tried to make him notice me. I worshipped him in secret, or what I thought was secret, although everyone at the mission knew."

Again she paused. Even though it had been seven years, this next chapter in her life was one she couldn't discuss in detail. It was still too traumatic.

"Mary Beth? If you'd rather not go on . . ."

Sweet, thoughtful Don. How like him to feel her pain.

"Thanks," she said, "but I can't banish the dream unless I get the whole experience out of my system. A little more than a year after Flynn came into my life, there was a military takeover of the government, and the fighting extended to our isolated area. My parents and several others at the mission and clinic were killed. It . . . it was awful!"

She hid her face in her hands and struggled for control as that nightmarish carnage played out in her memory with total recall.

Peggy jumped up and came around the table to put her arms around Mary Beth. "Don't put yourself through this," she said softly. "We get the picture."

The comfort of Peggy's arms and tone helped to calm Mary Beth, and she lowered her hands and raised her head. "Why don't you pour us another cup of coffee while I take a quick break. I'll be okay, honest."

Within a few minutes they'd moved into the living room. Don and Mary Beth sat on the brown sofa, which had been cleared of the bedding Don had used during the night, and Peggy curled up in the matching chair.

"You can imagine the state I was in," Mary Beth continued, anxious to get this over with. "Flynn and I were away from the mission at the time, and when we heard the shouts and the gunshots, it was too late to help. We hid out in the forest until it was over, or we'd have been killed, too. Afterward I was in shock and he took charge."

Her throat was dry and her heart pounded as she relived the horror. "The military held the airports, and getting out of the country was almost impossible. The American government insisted that all American citizens be allowed to return to the United States. Flynn and I managed to get to the nearest airport with just the clothes we were wearing."

Peggy shuddered. "Well, at least you got out."

Mary Beth shook her head. "I'm afraid it wasn't quite that easy. Flynn had his passport and birth certificate, but mine had been destroyed, and I had no way of proving that I was an American citizen. Worse yet, I was only seventeen, a minor, and I'd been in the country so long that I talked and behaved more like a native than a foreigner. The soldiers thought Flynn was trying to sneak me out, and they wouldn't let me leave."

"Good heavens, how did you escape?"

"I didn't exactly escape," Mary Beth explained. "We were afraid the fighting would begin again at any moment, and the only way I could leave quickly was as Flynn's wife, and therefore his dependent."

This time it was Don who spoke. "Dammit, that doesn't make any sense. Why didn't he become your legal guardian? After all, you were little more than a child."

Again Mary Beth pushed her hair back from her face. "Very few things make sense in Central America during an uprising. It would have taken weeks for an application for guardianship to be completed, and the country was in the middle of a war. The army was making its own laws, and the soldiers were willing to accept a wedding license as identification, so we didn't argue. We were married and flew to San Antonio, Texas, the same day.''

"What a hellish experience,'' Peggy said. "I'm surprised you can talk about it so calmly.''

Mary Beth grimaced and held out a trembling hand. "I'm not at all calm, as you can see, and at the time I was stunned and terrified, little more than a zombie. Flynn literally led me through those several days. I did anything he told me to without question. He seemed to know exactly how to get us to safety, although he told me afterward that he was putting up a bold front and hoping to bluff his way through.''

She sighed, and her voice dropped to a husky murmur. "He did, and he did it magnificently.''

Don captured the hand she'd held out. Her first instinct was to pull away, but he was offering comfort and she couldn't refuse his gesture.

"What happened when you got back to the States?'' He clasped her hand in his big one. "Didn't you say Flynn was engaged to another woman? How did she take the news that he was married to you?''

Mary Beth tried to relax, but her nerves were strung tight. "I don't know how she took it. Flynn never told me. We landed in Texas and went to a hotel where we slept around the clock. When we wakened, he said he'd escort me to whichever relative I wanted to stay with.''

She laughed, but her laughter was self-demeaning. "You can imagine his shock when I told him I didn't have any relatives, not even a great-aunt or a distant cousin.''

"I was all alone in the world except for my brand-new husband."

Peggy sipped her coffee. "I gather that the marriage hadn't been . . . I mean—"

"The marriage hadn't been consummated," Mary Beth finished for her. "You have to understand that I wasn't thinking straight, and I was unbelievably naive. My intellectual education had been excellent. I even knew all about sex and birthing babies. It's an uncomplicated way of life in the back country, and I'd observed both firsthand, but all I knew about love was what I'd read in the carefully chosen books available at the mission. *Cinderella*, *Jane Eyre*, *Romeo and Juliet*. Highly stylized fantasies of tender, undying passion. I'd been taught that marriage is forever, and it never occurred to me that mine wasn't intended to be."

Don released her hand and picked up his mug. "But you indicated that the two of you were living together intimately when you found him making out with the other woman," he said.

Oh, my, yes, they'd lived together *very* intimately for more than three and a half years, and for her their passion had been all-consuming.

"When Flynn found out I was all alone and totally unprepared to be on my own, he took me with him to Baltimore. His father, Dr. Edward Warren, is a nationally known cardiologist and was one of the pioneers in open-heart surgery. He's on the staff at Johns Hopkins Medical Center, and at first we stayed with Ed and Joan, Flynn's mother, in their big, beautiful home. They welcomed me warmly, and Vanessa was never mentioned. She was also a physician and practicing in Philadelphia, about three hundred miles away, so I didn't meet her until a couple of years later."

Peggy shook her head. "I think I've missed something along the way. Surely when Flynn told his parents about you, they must have mentioned his fiancée."

Mary Beth shrugged. "Again, I was never told. Flynn had called his parents and explained the situation before we left Texas, but I wasn't included in the conversation. He made the call from the lobby of the hotel, and then told me what he and they had decided to do."

"And you let him get away with treating you like that?" There was outrage in Peggy's tone.

"Ah, Peg, my liberated friend, not all cultures are like America," Mary Beth said patiently. "The country where I grew up was male dominated. The men made the decisions, and their wives did what they were told. That's the way I thought marriages worked. It's incredible how narrow my view of life was. Flynn acted like a guardian, and it took me a long time to realize that I had rights, too."

"I loved my husband. He was my whole life, and I would have done anything to make him happy."

"Were you happy, Mary Beth?" It was Don who spoke.

She answered without a moment's hesitation. "Yes. Oh, yes. Especially after we . . ." She stopped, flustered. "Uh . . . we didn't consummate our marriage for almost six months."

She held up her hands as they both looked at her with astonishment. "I know, you're wondering why I put up with that. Actually, I did approach Flynn once. He was amorous and tender, and now I realize that he was tempted almost beyond endurance, but he explained that I was very young and our marriage had been hurried. He needed to be sure I knew what I wanted before he took my virginity."

She saw the disbelief in their expressions and hurried on. "I believed him then, and I believe him now. When he finally did come to me, it was out of desperation, and even in my innocence I understood how difficult his restraint had been for him. It was the most beautiful experience I'd ever known.''

She leaned her head back and closed her eyes. *Beautiful* seemed inadequate to describe the wonder of their lovemaking, either the first careful deflowering or the hundreds of subsequent expressions of their ardor. He'd always taken the time to arouse her slowly with tender kisses, soft caresses and loving words, then built the tension to a mindless urgency before joining her in the flight over the rainbow to the never-never land of splintering ecstasy.

Don didn't try to hide his agitation. "If things were that great between you, then why did he chuck it all for another woman? Sounds like you were every man's dream of the perfect wife, especially in bed.''

Again she felt the cursed blush. "Oh, well, yes, he liked that, but I don't have to tell you, Don, that a man can have a satisfactory physical relationship with a woman without being in love with her. Unfortunately, it took me a long time to learn that. Meanwhile Flynn went into practice with two other pediatricians, and we bought a house not far from his parents and settled down together.

"I thought our marriage had been made in heaven. I wanted a baby right away, but he said I was too young. He wanted me to go to college as my parents had planned. I enrolled at the university as an education major and graduated with honors just weeks before..." Her voice broke and she tried again. "Before I discovered that Flynn was still in love with another woman.''

Don muttered a harsh oath and stood up. Peggy shot him a disapproving look and leaned forward. "Mary Beth, as a woman, I find it hard to believe that you had no inkling that your husband wasn't in love with you. Surely there must have been signs.''

Mary Beth nodded. ''There were, but I refused to recognize them. He was always patient and kind, but he continued to treat me like an adolescent. At times he was a pain, telling me what I could and couldn't do, making sure I studied hard and did my homework, but as I've said, I grew up in a culture where husbands were overbearing. I didn't want to cross him and risk his displeasure.''

Don muttered another oath from across the room, then apologized before his sister could scold him.

Mary Beth grinned. ''Just because I go to church every Sunday doesn't mean I've never heard men swear,'' she said to Peggy.

Her grin disappeared as she continued. ''As Flynn became more involved with his practice, he worked long hours and spent less time with me. Our lovemaking became more hurried and less frequent, so that by the time I caught him with Vanessa he was spending little time at home. We didn't quarrel, so I never suspected another woman. I just accepted the fact that he was very busy and tried not to make too many demands.''

Peggy groaned. ''I hope the time you spent in Madrid showed you the error of your ways.''

''Oh, yes. Once I was on my own and had to do things for myself, I became liberated quickly. By then I'd lived in Baltimore and finished college so, once I was no longer concerned about pleasing Flynn, I found that I rather liked being independent.''

She glanced at her watch and was surprised to find that she'd been telling her story for almost two hours.

''Good grief, I didn't realize I'd been rattling on for so long. Anyway, you know the rest. After I'd filed for divorce, I went to Spain where I put my education, and my knowledge of the Spanish language, to good use teaching in an orphanage on the outskirts of Madrid. Eight months ago I returned to this country and started teaching English as a second language to Spanish-speaking students here in San Diego, where I also had the great good fortune to make friends with the two of you.''

She stood and headed for the kitchen. ''How about some breakfast? I'll cook.''

''Hey, wait a minute,'' Don protested. ''You didn't tell us how Flynn reacted when you walked in on him and Vanessa, or what he thought about the divorce.''

Mary Beth stopped, but didn't turn around. ''I'd rather not discuss that now. Maybe later.''

Chapter Two

On Monday morning Mary Beth parked her 1986 silver-gray Nissan Sentra in the small area of paved school yard reserved for teachers' cars. She dropped her keys into her purse and turned to Peggy, who was sitting in the passenger seat. "Do you ever get the impression that El Dorado Elementary School is a tad low on the school board's priority list?" Her tone was appropriately sarcastic.

"Humph." Peggy grunted with disgust as she viewed the peeling paint and cracked pavement. "I doubt if the board even knows it's still in the system. The staff and the PTA have been petitioning for years for a cafeteria, but we'd be happy if they'd just bring the buildings up to standard."

The school where both Mary Beth and Peggy taught was one of the oldest in the city and was situated in a predominantly Hispanic neighborhood. Most of the residents didn't speak English well enough to communicate effectively, and Mary Beth's classes in English as a second language were filled to overflowing.

The two women got out of the car and walked in the direction of the portable classrooms. "California has strong desegregation laws," Mary Beth observed, "so how come El Dorado Elementary is seventy percent Hispanic? If we had a better ethnic balance, more parents who understood and spoke English, we'd have a better chance of making our problems known."

Peggy shrugged. "There are lots of excuses. Not enough money, transportation problems, a shortage of teachers, but you're right. Until the parents understand that their children are entitled to better conditions and demand them, other schools will get priority." She turned to her left. "See you at lunch," she said, and walked toward her classroom.

Mary Beth nodded and turned right just as a childish voice called, *"Maestra. Maestra. Hola!"* and a black-haired, black-eyed little girl of six threw herself at her teacher and hugged her around the waist.

Mary Beth laughed and hugged the child back. "Hello, Juanita. My, don't you look pretty this morning, but have you forgotten that we only speak English at school?"

The dark head nodded. "I am sorry, *señorita . . . Miss* Warren," she said, her words heavily accented. "I was *excitado . . .* excited."

Mary Beth hadn't asked for her maiden name back, and used the title *Ms.*, which the children translated as *Miss*. She hugged the little one again, then took her hand and walked with her to their classroom.

For at least the millionth time in the past three years, she wished there was some way she could thank Flynn for providing her with the education that made it possible for her to work with underprivileged children the way her parents had. She was sure it was what she'd been born to do.

That evening Peggy cooked dinner. Mary Beth was cleaning up the kitchen afterward when Peggy spoke from behind her. "Mary Beth, there's something in the newspaper I think you should see."

Neither of the women had had time to read *The Tribune* or listen to the news earlier in their busy day, and there was something in Peggy's tone that sent a chill of foreboding through Mary Beth.

She turned, and her friend's troubled expression told her she wasn't overreacting. After wiping her wet hands down her jeans, she reached out and took the paper. It was turned to page two, and the first thing she saw was a picture of Edward Warren, Flynn's father.

The headline read, "Doctor Who Pioneered in Open-Heart Surgery Dies."

She felt the grief like a blow to her midsection, and her gasp was a cry of pain. Edward, the gruff bear of a man who had taken her into his home and his heart, even though her marriage to his son caused such upheaval in all their lives. The father-in-law who had become almost as dear to her as her own father had been.

Peggy was beside her, an arm around her waist, urging her toward a chair. "I should have known better than to spring it on you that way," she muttered as Mary Beth sat down. "Now, take a deep breath and I'll get you some brandy."

Mary Beth read the first two paragraphs of the article and learned that Edward had died in a hospital early Sunday morning at the age of seventy-one.

"I know you don't drink," Peggy said as she set a snifter in front of her, "but make an exception this time. Just sip it slowly."

Rather than argue, Mary Beth took a small swallow and let the golden liquor trickle down her throat and loosen the knot of tears that had formed there.

"Thanks," she said. "I suppose it shouldn't have come as such a shock, but I never thought of Ed in terms of death. He was such a vital, energetic man. So full of life and determined to save it in others...."

Her voice broke, and she took another sip of the brandy. "Poor Joan, his wife. She must be devastated. And Flynn..."

Mary Beth closed her eyes and fought for control. Flynn and his father had been so close. Even though he had two sisters, there was a special tie from being the only son. He'd followed Edward into the medical profession, and his love and respect for his famous father had been strong and deep.

Peggy's voice brought her out of her reverie. "Are you going to the memorial service?"

Mary Beth opened her eyes and looked at her friend. "The memorial service? No, I couldn't possibly go back to Baltimore. When I returned to this country, I deliberately settled on the West Coast, as far as I could get from there. I don't want them to know where I am."

Peggy looked startled. "You mean they don't know you're in San Diego?"

Mary Beth shook her head. "No. When I left the country three years ago after filing for divorce, I didn't tell anybody where I was going. I haven't been in contact with the Warrens or anyone else in Baltimore since. There was no need to be, and I didn't want to hear about Flynn's marriage to Vanessa or the birth of any children they may have had.''

Peggy looked almost as shocked as Mary Beth felt, but Mary Beth had no idea what it was she'd said that upset the other woman so.

''Peg? What's the matter?''

''Mary Beth, didn't you finish reading that article in the paper?'' Peggy's tone was soft.

''No.'' Mary Beth glanced at the newspaper lying beside her glass on the table. ''It's continued on another page. I haven't gotten to it yet.''

Peggy reached over, picked up the paper and turned to where the article was continued. ''I'd better read it to you,'' she said. ''It tells about his career at Johns Hopkins, then toward the end it says, 'Dr. Warren retired two years ago and moved back to La Jolla, California, where both he and his wife had been born and raised—''

Mary Beth gasped as still another shock rocked her. La Jolla! But that was a part of San Diego! An affluent resort area along the coast, popular with executives and professionals as a retirement community.

Peggy held up her hand and continued reading. ''He is survived by his wife, Joan, two daughters, Gwen Thomas of Baltimore, Maryland, and Carol Adams of Falls Church, Virginia, and a son, Dr. Flynn Warren, *who is also a resident of La Jolla*.''

Peggy emphasized the last few words, but Mary Beth would have felt the blow of them if they'd been whispered. At first she felt numb, then the rising heat of angry disbelief. ''That can't be true,'' she snapped as she rose from her chair and grabbed the paper out of Peggy's hands. ''It must be a misprint.''

Anxiously she scanned the page, but even as the blurred print came into focus, she knew there had been no mistake. How could she have forgotten that Edward and Joan had been born and raised in California? Talk about a Freudian slip. Her psyche had really tripped her up this time!

Peggy stood and pointed over Mary Beth's shoulder to the sentence in question. "It's right there," she said calmly. "It also says a memorial service will be held in La Jolla at 11:00 a.m. on Wednesday. Since that's just a few miles up the coast, I suggest that you plan to attend. You'll always regret it if you don't."

Mary Beth was dressed and waiting half an hour before Don was scheduled to pick her up. She sat in the living room of the apartment, leafing through a magazine, but had no idea what was in it.

Darn, how had she gotten herself into this? When Peggy first suggested she go to Edward's memorial service, she'd refused. It had taken her too long to recover from her unfortunate marriage to Flynn Warren. Even now it was a tenuous recovery, and she wasn't going to place herself in jeopardy by deliberately coming in contact with him and his new wife.

It wasn't until the first shock had worn off that she began to have second thoughts. Edward had been very dear to her, and she knew he must have been terribly upset when she left so suddenly without a word to anyone.

If she was given a chance to do it over again, she'd do it differently, but at the time, in her pain and humiliation, she'd acted hastily. Now she'd never be able to tell him how much she loved him for his willingness to assume the role of the father she'd lost. How much his gruff affection, his emotional support and his determination that she remain a part of his family even though she was divorcing his son had meant to her.

Peggy was right. She'd never forgive herself if she didn't pay her last respects. She blinked back tears and stifled a sob as she got up and walked to the window. Enough of that. She wasn't going to make a fool of herself by breaking down, especially in public.

Peggy and Don had convinced her that by arriving at the time when the crowd would be the thickest, and sitting at the back of the church, she could attend the services without being seen by the family. Don had even volunteered to go with her and give her the moral support she so badly needed. She'd halfheartedly tried to talk him out of it, knowing he'd have to take time off from his job, but he'd insisted. She was glad he had. If he wasn't coming to take her, she was afraid she would change her mind and go back to school instead.

Dr. Flynn Warren stood at the long window in the church parlor and watched through the sheer curtain as the mass of solemn, well-dressed men and women filed into the sanctuary. They weren't all mourners. Many were media photographers and reporters eager to record the dignitaries who arrived in chauffeur-driven limousines.

Inwardly he cringed as he thought of having to greet all these people after the service, and again later the hundred or so who had been invited to the house for a buffet lunch. Flynn knew that his father would have preferred a small private funeral, and it would have been easier on the family members, but that was nearly impossible for a man of Edward's stature in his profession.

Flynn's gaze swept over the beautifully kept lawn at the front of the big modern glass-and-wood church building, an architectural style popular in Southern California. The influx had thinned as the time to start grew nearer, and

Flynn was about to turn away when one young couple walking up the sidewalk caught his eye.

His whole body tensed and tingled as the cursedly familiar shock caught him off guard. Quickly he looked away from the woman on the arm of the man.

Damn! When was he going to stop seeing Mary Beth in every beautiful blonde he glimpsed? He'd hoped that when he'd sold his practice in Baltimore and moved three thousand miles away to California that his persistent subconscious would realize that he wasn't going to find her, and stop looking.

It hadn't happened, and he couldn't stop himself from seeking this one out again. The curtain blurred his vision enough to make it difficult to see facial features from this distance, but the sharp tingle of awareness that always shook him when this happened didn't go away.

There was a certain familiarity about the high breasts, tiny waist and rounded hips that the well-cut navy-blue suit she wore couldn't conceal. And the hair. Although it was drawn back and worn close to her head, the wispy bangs and the shimmering golden color were almost identical to the way Mary Beth's had been.

Again Flynn looked away. This was ridiculous. Why was he standing here hallucinating about a woman who disliked him so much that she'd run away rather than have anything more to do with him? His grief for his father must have unhinged him!

Even so, he had to be sure. He drew the curtain back and looked again at the couple, although he was only marginally aware of the man. This time they were close enough for him to see the young lady in exquisite detail.

Flynn stumbled and clutched at the curtain. Her clear, creamy complexion highlighted an oval face with a gently rounded jaw and chin. Almond-shaped blue eyes were fringed with thick dark lashes and gently arched brows. But it was her mouth that caused his knees to tremble. He could almost feel its full sweetness moving under his own.

Dear Lord, it *was* Mary Beth!

He whirled around and ran toward the nearest exit.

Rich, full tones from the magnificent pipe organ filled the sanctuary of the church as Mary Beth and Don followed the usher a few steps down the aisle to a row where there were still two empty seats together. They were at the back of the cavernous oblong room lined on either side with priceless stained glass windows depicting the scriptures.

After squeezing past several occupied seats, they'd settled down and were reading the printed order of worship they'd been given when Mary Beth felt a hand on her shoulder. Startled, she looked up into the face that was engraved in her soul. Flynn!

His fingers tightened on her shoulder. "Come with me, Mary Elizabeth."

Mary Beth was speechless as she felt the blood drain from her face. How had Flynn spotted her in this crowd, and what did he want? His voice was cool, and he'd called her Mary Elizabeth. He only called her that when he was angry with her. Was he going to ask her to leave?"

"I want you to come with me," he said again, but this time Don intervened.

"Is something wrong?" Don asked politely, his tone was equally cool.

"Mrs. Warren is sitting in the wrong seat," Flynn said. "She belongs with the family."

The family! He wanted her to sit up front with him and Vanessa? "No, I couldn't," she blurted louder than she'd intended, then lowered her voice. "I prefer to sit here."

His grip on her shoulder tightened again, and he leaned closer. "Please don't make a scene. Just come with me so we can start the services."

She looked around and saw the choir was in the loft at the front, and the black-robed minister was standing at the altar. Everything was waiting on her.

Her stomach muscles knotted, and she looked at Don. "It's all right," he assured her. "Go with him. I'll stay here and wait for you."

She stood and once more squeezed past the occupied seats to walk in a daze beside Flynn down the outside aisle to the front pew where the family was seated.

As they rounded the corner of the first row, she saw his sisters, Gwen and Carol, sitting with their husbands and their mother, Joan. Joan looked up directly at Mary Beth. Her patrician face, lovely even in grief, was blank for a moment, then a look of astonishment swept over it as she held out her arms.

Mary Beth sank to her knees in front of the woman who had been her second mother, and they clasped each other tightly. "Oh, Joan," Mary Beth murmured, "I'm so sorry. So very, very sorry."

Her words had a double meaning. Sorry Edward was dead, and sorry she hadn't contacted them in all these years.

The organist switched to a familiar anthem, and the choir began to sing. She felt Flynn's strong hands lift her gently and seat her, then he took the space between her and his mother while the music swelled and ebbed.

It was only then that she realized there was no sign of Vanessa. As discreetly as possible she looked around, but since they were in the front row, she could only see those on either side of her. The people across the center aisle were strangers.

Where was Vanessa? Surely she wouldn't let her husband go through such an emotionally devastating experience without her there to comfort and support him.

She stole a glance at Flynn, who was wedged in so close beside her that their arms, hips and thighs touched. Warmth radiated through her from the contact, and she clasped her hands in her lap to keep from touching him on the leg, caressing it the way he used to like her to.

There were shallow lines at the corners of his eyes and mouth, but she could still feel the hard muscles through the fine wool of his coat and trousers. His dark-blond hair was cut short on the sides and back, but the golden highlights were still there.

Always slender, he seemed even more so, but it only served to emphasize his almost perfect features. High cheekbones, broad brow, sculptured nose and the stubborn set of his strong chin.

He looked pale, and his deep-set brown eyes were filled with sadness. On the other side of him, Joan and her daughters sobbed quietly, but Flynn was stoic. Mary Beth had never seen him cry, and even now the only overt signs of his distress were the tenseness of his carriage and his clenched fists.

Why wasn't Vanessa here to help him through this difficult time?

Mary Beth hadn't been paying attention to the service, but now she noticed that the minister was speaking. He praised Edward's medical skill, his kindness and generosity. He told of Edward's deep love for his wife and children, his pride in his sons-in-law and grandchildren.

Mary Beth thought she'd cried all the tears she had for her dear friend and second father in the privacy of her room, but she was wrong. They welled in her eyes and spilled down her cheeks, and when she noticed the pulse pounding in Flynn's clenched jaws, she couldn't stand his anguish any longer. Reaching over, she laid her palm on his fist.

He opened his fingers and grasped her hand, then lifted it to his mouth. His caressing lips sent waves of pleasure down her arm, melting the resistance that had pricked briefly at her conscience. After a moment he lowered their clasped hands to his chest and held them there over the unsteady beat of his heart. She put her forehead on his shoulder and let the tears come.

When the congregation stood for the closing hymn, she pulled away from Flynn and groped in her purse for a tissue.

After the benediction the ushers came to the front row, and Mary Beth realized that they were going to escort the family members out first so they could greet the others as they emerged.

Flynn looked at her. "Will you come with me?"

She blinked. He wanted her to stand and accept condolences with the family? How did he intend to introduce her? *This is Mary Beth, my first wife? She's standing in temporarily for the second?*

Her gaze collided with his, and she was almost sure that his eyes were pleading with her.

No, that couldn't be. She was reading his signals wrong again. She didn't dare trust her instincts where he was concerned. For the four years of their marriage, she'd been so sure she could interpret his wants and needs correctly, but she'd never picked up on the fact that he was still in love with Vanessa.

She'd been such a fool, but no more.

"No, Flynn," she said, "I don't belong there. Besides, Don has to get back to work."

He frowned. "Ah, yes, the man you're with. Tell him to go on. I'll take you wherever you want to go later, but we have to talk first."

He must have seen that she was about to refuse again, because he said the one thing she couldn't refute. "Surely you owe me that much."

Yes, she did. She owed it to him to explain why she'd disappeared without a trace at the time when he'd been trying so hard to make things right again between them.

It had puzzled her when he'd insisted so passionately that he didn't want a divorce, until she realized that he still thought of her as the naive teenager who needed to be taken care of. That was when she'd decided to get out of his life completely and start taking responsibility for herself. As long as he'd known where she was and what she was doing, he'd have felt responsible for her.

Before she could answer, Joan reached for her hand and murmured, "Oh, my dear, I can't tell you how grateful I am that you've finally returned. We'll see you at the house later."

Again she and Mary Beth embraced, and Mary Beth acknowledged defeat. "All right, I'll wait," she said to Flynn, then sat back down while the family members filed out, followed row by row by the rest of the mourners.

After a few minutes Don came down and sat beside her. They watched quietly as the big church slowly emptied, then Don spoke. "Are you okay?"

She nodded. "Yes. I'm sorry I left you sitting all by yourself. I wasn't thinking straight."

"Hey, no problem. Your ex-husband seemed awfully glad to see you." He took her hand and held it. "I still find it hard to believe that any man would cheat on you."

"Flynn didn't," she said, then hurried to explain when she saw his look of confusion. "That is, not really. He swore he'd never been unfaithful to me, that he hadn't been intimate with Vanessa since he'd returned to this country with me as his wife, and I believe him. Flynn is a very moral man. I didn't leave him because he'd broken his vows to me, but because I couldn't bear the thought of him feeling he had to live with me even though he was in love with another woman."

Her voice trembled, and she took a deep breath. "I owed the man my life, the least I could do was give him his freedom."

Anxious to change the subject, Mary Beth looked at her watch. It was noon, and although she'd taken the whole day off, Don was due back at his job after lunch. She turned to him. "You don't need to wait for me," she said. "I need to talk to Flynn. I'll call a cab when I'm ready to leave."

Don seemed uncertain. "Look, honey, I helped Peggy talk you into coming here, and I said I'd escort you. I'm not going to desert you just because it's taking a little longer than we'd figured."

"I'll be all right," she said, and knew it was the truth. "The worst that could happen did—I came face-to-face with Flynn and survived. Apparently Vanessa isn't here, so that's one confrontation I've been spared. I'll try to make my peace with these people, and then maybe I can get my ill-fated marriage and divorce in perspective and banish the nightmare."

"Well, if you're sure." He consulted his own watch. "I'll have time for a quick lunch if I leave now...."

She squeezed his hand before pulling hers away. "I'm sure, Don, really. Thanks again for coming with me."

It took all of half an hour for the building to empty completely while the hundreds of people stopped to offer sympathy and share their favorite memories of Edward with his wife and children. Mary Beth sat quietly, gathering strength from the peaceful surroundings. The organist continued his concert, and the sacred music was soothing and restful.

She was sitting with her head down and her eyes closed when she felt, rather than heard, the footsteps coming down the thickly carpeted center aisle. She looked around and saw Flynn hurrying toward her.

Standing, she took a few steps, and then she was in his arms. He held her close in an almost frantic embrace, and she clung as the familiar feel and scent and touch of him overpowered her and sent the blood racing through her veins.

Her puritan conscience was screaming warnings, but it didn't have a chance against the magnetism that radiated between them. She couldn't deny him or herself the comfort they needed from each other.

"Mary Beth," he murmured huskily. "Where have you been? I nearly lost my mind when you disappeared like that. If you wanted to punish me, you succeeded."

Punish him? She hadn't wanted to punish him, she'd just wanted to set him free to resume the life he'd planned with Vanessa.

She winced as the name conjured a picture of the woman—tall, stately, with short straight black hair and gray eyes that for just a fraction of a second on that night three years ago had held triumph as she and Flynn jumped apart upon hearing Mary Beth's cry of surprise and pain.

Vanessa, who was now Flynn's wife!

With a gasp of dismay for her weakness, Mary Beth pulled roughly away from him and retreated several steps backward. "What makes you think I was trying to punish you?" she asked heatedly. "I was just giving you the only thing you'd ever wanted from me, your freedom to marry Vanessa. So where is she? Aren't you concerned about what she'll think when she hears that I was sitting with you during the funeral?''

She knew she was being too loud and too quarrelsome for the hallowed confines of the church, but she couldn't seem to tone it down.

Flynn stared at her as though he didn't understand what she was talking about. ''What does Vanessa have to do with Dad's funeral?''

Now it was her turn to stare. She'd believed him when he told her he'd never committed adultery with the other woman, even though he admitted being guilty of sharing kisses with her, because she'd known him to be an honorable man. But now he was implying that there was no reason for his present wife to object to his association with his ex-wife!

''I'll admit I was appallingly innocent when we were together,'' she said impatiently, ''but even then I knew that no decent man would seek comfort from his ex-wife at a family funeral just because his present wife was unable to attend.'' She looked around. ''Where is she? Why isn't she here?''

Flynn's gaze searched Mary Beth's face, and his voice was soft when he spoke. ''Your lawyer was telling me the truth. He didn't know where you were. You haven't been in touch with him, have you?''

She blinked. This conversation seemed to be going around in circles. ''I was in Spain for a couple of years, and now I'm teaching in San Diego. As for Mr. Yeager, no, I haven't been in touch with him. You and I worked out the terms of the divorce before I left. Now, if you'll excuse me, I'll say goodbye to your mother and sisters. Then I really must be going.''

She turned to leave, but Flynn's quiet voice stopped her. "I'm not married to Vanessa, Mary Beth, and I never have been. Last I heard she'd married a widower with two teenage children. Now suppose you tell me who Don is and what he means to you." A sudden look of dismay crossed his features. "My God, you're not married to him, are you?"

Chapter Three

Mary Beth was too stunned to reply. A tidal wave of relief swept over her as his words finally registered. Flynn hadn't remarried! But why?

"It...it never occurred to me that you and Vanessa hadn't gotten married as soon as you were free," she finally said.

"And you never bothered to contact me and ask, did you?" His tone was accusing.

She bristled. "No, I didn't. I assumed that your feelings for her were so deep that they had become unmanageable. I thought you were too honorable a man to indulge in light flirtations with other women when you were married to me. Apparently I was mistaken."

"Mary Beth!" The strain on his pale face deepened as he reacted with incredulity. "You can't honestly believe that...."

She was immediately sorry. He had all the stress he could handle; it was unforgivable of her to add to it.

Reaching out to him, she put her hand on his arm. "No, Flynn. You're right, I don't. I'm sorry." Her tone was husky with regret. "I don't know what went wrong, but I do know that you must have loved her very much. I just hope that you didn't lose her again because of me."

With a groan he took her in his arms and buried his face in the curve of her neck. "Oh, my God, Mary Beth," he murmured brokenly, "how can I ever make you understand...?"

She held him and stroked her fingers through his short thick hair. This time she embraced him without guilt, and her heart swelled with the joy of reunion, however short. She knew she was setting herself up for more heartbreak, but the sensation of his head beneath her caressing fingers, his face nestled at the side of her throat and his long length pressed tightly into her soft curves was worth every sleepless night and tormented day she'd have to suffer later.

"I do understand," she said gently. "I've never blamed you. I blamed myself for being so naive. It's just that today I'm unstrung with the shock of seeing you and your family again. I hadn't intended to. I thought you'd be married and have a child. Don said we could leave by a side door and not have to see you."

At the mention of Don, Flynn straightened and stepped away from her. "I'm afraid we got off the subject of Don," he snapped. "Who is he, and what is he to you?"

She bit back an equally snappish retort and explained patiently. "His name is Donald MacGregor. He's the brother of my apartment mate, Margaret MacGregor, and he's my dear friend."

Flynn glared. "How dear?"

She gasped, and when she spoke, her voice was tight with resistance. "Very dear."

He grasped her shoulders. "Are you sleeping with him?"

Mary Beth had never seen Flynn so agitated, and, even as her temper flared it occurred to her that the church was no place for this conversation. What difference did it make to him whom she was sleeping with? Maybe he thought she should have joined a nunnery after he was through with her.

"That's none of your business," she said angrily.

"The hell it's not. You're my wife." His face was no longer pale, but flushed.

"Not anymore," she reminded him, appalled at his gall in thinking she was somehow still his possession. "And what I do or who I sleep with is none of your concern." She picked up her purse from the pew. "If you'll show me where I can find a phone, I'll call a cab and go home."

Flynn ran his hands over his face and took a deep breath. "I'm sorry," he said wearily. "I'm handling this badly, but I've just about reached the end of my endurance. This past week has been torture, and then when I looked out the window and saw you coming up the walk, I...I think my whole nervous system short-circuited. I don't seem to be able to function properly."

He reached out and cupped her face with his hands. "You've grown up," he said with a touch of sadness as his gaze roamed over her. "You've still got the same firm chin, delicate nose and ripe rosy lips that taste of sweetness and passion and woman, but where is my innocent little girl? She no longer looks out of those magnificent blue eyes. Did I destroy her that night three years ago?"

Mary Beth was mesmerized by his soft voice and his searching gaze that touched each of her features separately as he spoke of them.

She ran the tip of her tongue over her lips before she replied. "I suppose you did, but it was past time for her to go. I couldn't stay childlike forever."

She felt his glance pulling her to him, and knew that in another second his mouth would cover hers and make her whole again after so many lonely years. With no will to resist, she watched his face lower slowly until she could feel his clean, cool breath on her overheated skin. Her trembling lips parted to receive him just as the organ music stopped, leaving a roar of silence as distracting as a clap of thunder.

Instinctively they jumped apart as the organist stood and gathered up his music.

Flynn muttered something under his breath and took her arm. "Come on, let's get out of here." His voice was laced with frustration. "There's a car waiting to take us to the house."

She had to hurry to keep up with him as he strode up the long aisle. "What house?"

"My parents...uh...my mother's house," he said as they came out of the dimness into the sunlight of the glassed-in foyer. "We've arranged a buffet lunch."

She remembered Joan saying something about seeing her at the house later, but the idea of being confronted by his family en masse was daunting. "Please, Flynn, I'd rather not. I need time to pull myself together before I face the rest of your family with explanations."

He pushed open the glass door and stepped back to let her precede him outside. "You've had three years to yourself, and I'm not going to let you out of my sight again until we've had a good, long talk. Besides, Mother's expecting you."

Before she could think of an argument, he'd helped her
into the back seat of a black limousine, then crawled in
beside her.

Mary Beth leaned against the soft leather seat and was
enveloped in comfort. She'd never ridden in a limo before. When they were married, Flynn had always preferred to drive himself, and in Spain she'd ridden public
transportation or walked.

He took her hand and held it on the seat between them.
"Forgive me for being so overbearing," he said contritely. "I promise that after today I'll do better."

Did that mean that he wanted to see her again? The fact
that he hadn't married again had totally thrown her. She
didn't know what to expect.

"Oh, Flynn. I, of all people, understand what you're
going through. Have you forgotten how traumatized I was
when Dad and Mother were killed?"

He squeezed her hand. "That was different."

"The circumstances were different, but if it hadn't been
for you, I'd never have gotten out of the country alive. I
couldn't even think, let alone make decisions. If there's
anything I can do to make your loss more bearable, I
will."

For the first time, a ghost of a smile hovered around the
corners of his mouth. "You'd better be careful what you
offer. I might take you up on it."

Before she could decide whether or not he was teasing,
the limo stopped and the driver got out and opened the
door.

Mary Beth gasped when she saw where they were. It was
a tree-lined street of big homes high on a cliff overlooking the ocean. The curbs were lined with luxury cars, and
the house in front of them was overflowing with people.

Inside, a buffet of cold cuts, salads, hot dishes and desserts had been set up on long tables in the dining room, and the guests mingled in friendly conversation. Flynn's sisters were stationed in the roomy entryway, greeting people as they arrived. Carol, the youngest at age thirty-two, welcomed Mary Beth enthusiastically with a hug, but Gwen, four years older than Flynn, was coolly impersonal and offered only a handshake.

Mary Beth felt the chill and was quite sure that dealing with Gwen wasn't going to be pleasant.

Flynn asked about his mother and was told she was in the living room. They found her there accepting condolences graciously. Flynn took his place beside Joan and joined the conversation. He tried to hold on to Mary Beth, but she murmured something about going to the powder room and slipped away. She didn't feel right acting as a member of the family.

She wandered alone through the downstairs rooms of the beautiful home. It was not as large as the one Edward and Joan had owned in Baltimore, but newer and more modern. The panoramic view of La Jolla's rocky coast and fine beaches from the picture windows at the back of the house was spectacular.

It was there that Gwen Warren Thomas found her. "Well, Mary Beth," she said, "I gather you've decided to come home." There was no welcome in her tone.

Mary Beth shook her head without looking at Flynn's sister. "My home is an apartment in San Diego now," she said carefully. "I'm sorry if my being here today has upset you, Gwen."

"It was your abrupt leaving that upset me," Gwen answered. "How could you do such a thing to Flynn? I know he hurt you, but he didn't deserve to be put through three years of hell because of it."

Her tone was bitter, and Mary Beth didn't want to quarrel with her. Not here. Not now.

"It was never my intention to punish Flynn. I just wanted to get away so I wouldn't have to see him and Vanessa together. I loved him very much."

Gwen's features twisted with disbelief. "I think you're confusing love with dependency. You didn't love him—you needed him to take care of you. We all understood that when he married you in order to bring you back from Central America, but you never grew up."

Mary Beth cringed. Had everyone but she known that Flynn was just waiting for her to be independent so he could leave her?

Gwen didn't notice Mary Beth's distress as she continued. "If you'd truly loved him, you'd have released him from his vows before the marriage was consummated. After that, he felt that he was committed to you. He could no longer seek an annulment."

Mary Beth stifled a cry of anguish. Gwen was only telling her what she'd told herself so often in the past three years, but hearing it said by another made it even more unbearable. Why hadn't she seen it for herself? How could she not have known that Flynn was unhappy?

She put her forehead against the window and closed her eyes against the pain that seared her. Her fear that he had been wishing she was Vanessa all those times he'd made love to her so passionately had haunted her ever since that night she'd found them in each other's arms. She felt used, but she blamed herself instead of him. It gnawed at her self-respect and made her doubt her desirability as a woman.

Gwen's accusing voice droned on. "If you'd really loved him, you'd have had the decency to tell him you were going away, let him know where you would be living, what your plans were, and made a clean break of it. Instead you ran off without a word to anyone and nearly drove him crazy worrying about you.''

Mary Beth's shoulders shook with the effort she was making to hold back the sob that racked her, and she put her hand to her mouth just as a voice behind them intruded. ''What's going on here? Gwen, what are you saying?''

It was Flynn, and both women turned to face him. Mary Beth dropped her hand quickly, but knew her face still mirrored her torment. Flynn took one look at her and turned on his sister. ''Dammit, Gwen, I won't allow you to—''

''It's all right, Flynn,'' Mary Beth interrupted. ''We were just talking about... about your dad. This whole thing came as such a shock to me that I... I'm having difficulty dealing with my feelings.''

He looked doubtful, but let the subject drop as he put his arm around her waist. ''Most of the guests are gone now, so if you'll fix yourselves a plate of food and take it into the library, the family's gathering in there.''

Gwen started to walk away. ''Okay, I'll find Ken and the children—''

''Ken and Bill are rounding up all the kids and taking them to the zoo. They'll be gone all afternoon.'' Bill was their sister Carol's husband.

''Oh, good,'' Gwen answered, and left.

Fifteen minutes later Joan, her son, two daughters and Mary Beth were assembled in the book-lined library with plates of food and cups of strong, hot coffee. Mary Beth knew she was going to be expected to account for her whereabouts the past three years, and she'd limited her lunch to fruit salad and a slice of nut bread. If things got too rough, she didn't want much in her knotted stomach.

Flynn had seated her on the brown leather couch and himself beside her. Joan, looking exhausted, was ensconced in the rocking chair, and Gwen and Carol occupied the two lounge chairs.

It was Joan who started the discussion as she set aside her scarcely touched plate. "Mary Beth, I'm sure I speak for everyone when I say we're relieved and delighted to see you again. Do you mind explaining where you've been, and why you disappeared so abruptly?"

Mary Beth's stomach lurched, but she smiled as she, too, put her plate down. "Not at all," she answered, "but first let me say that I never intended to upset or worry any of you by leaving the way I did. It didn't occur to me that you would be especially concerned."

All of them protested at once. "How could you think that?"

"Of course we were worried!"

"Why?"

"My dear, you must have known we loved you!"

"I don't believe you."

The phrases were all jumbled together so she couldn't tell who said what. "Please..." She held up her hand for quiet. "I know you must think I was incredibly dense, but I'd had such a debilitating shock.... That is, I'd always thought Flynn was happy. I had no idea that he and Vanessa..."

She could feel herself falling apart, and she couldn't allow that. It was imperative that she prove to these nice people that she was a mature, well-adjusted adult now who could survive on her own.

"Mary Beth!" Flynn reached out to her, but she pulled away.

"No. I'm all right." She took a deep breath. "I'm sorry. Just please accept the fact that I was only trying to make things easier for all of you, but I messed up as usual.''

"Don't, sweetheart…" Again Flynn tried to touch her, but she rose to her feet and walked across the room to stand in front of the fireplace.

She squared her shoulders and cleared her throat. ''During my last semester at the university, one of the recruiters who came on campus was from an overseas agency that had openings for teachers proficient in Spanish to teach English in Spain. I didn't pay much attention at the time, but after I'd filed for divorce, I inquired further and found that I qualified. I applied and was accepted.''

"You mean you've been in Spain?" Joan asked.

"Yes. Madrid. I was a lay teacher in a church-run orphanage until early this year when I got homesick and came back to this country.''

"Why didn't you tell me your plans?" Flynn's voice was heavy with exasperation. "And why didn't you contact me immediately when you came back?''

She tucked a wisp of hair into her French braid. "You were insisting that you didn't want a divorce, but I'd finally grasped the fact that you were chained to me by a heavy sense of responsibility. I couldn't let you spend the rest of your life paying an obligation you never owed in the first place. The only way I could think of to prevent that was to get out of your life.''

With a moan Flynn balanced his elbows on his knees and bent over to drop his face into his hands. It took all of her strength to stand where she was and not go to him, put her arms around him and tell him how deeply she still loved him.

That would make her feel better, but it wasn't what he wanted to hear. It would only add to his sense of obligation. She had to make him understand that she was no longer the lost waif he'd married. If it meant letting him think she no longer needed him then that's what she'd have to do. She was such a wretched liar, though. Could she ever pull it off?

It was Gwen who unknowingly helped her. "If you were so anxious to stay out of his life and give him his freedom, why did you settle in San Diego when you came back to the States?" she asked, and her tone implied that she didn't believe Mary Beth's motives. "You must have known how easy it would be to run into him here."

Mary Beth sighed and shook her head. "I had no idea that Flynn and his parents were in California." She caught Gwen's look of disgust. "I know you don't believe me. Coincidences like that are just too pat, but I swear it never occurred to me that Flynn and his father weren't still practicing in Baltimore."

She began pacing in front of the hearth. "I chose San Diego because it was the farthest I could get from Baltimore and still be in the same country. I'd read about the program California has developed to teach English to the many Spanish-speaking children in the public schools down here. That's my area of expertise, and I was hired as soon as I applied. I was stunned when I read in Monday's paper that Flynn lived in La Jolla."

Gwen's expression indicated that she was still unconvinced. Flynn raised his head and looked at Mary Beth with an air of resignation. "Do you hate me so much that you couldn't even stand to live in the same part of the country with me?"

That did it. She couldn't bear to let him think such a monstrous distortion of the truth.

She crossed the room and sat down beside him, then put her hand to his cheek. "Oh, Flynn," she said shakily. "I

don't hate you. I never felt anything less than admiration
and respect for you." She reached out and caressed his
temple with supple fingers.

He caught her hand and brought the palm to his lips.
"And love?" he asked anxiously. "What about love,
Mary Beth?"

Involuntarily she shivered as he placed tiny kisses on her
sensitized skin. "Most assuredly, love," she murmured.
"I must have been the most lovesick girl who ever lost her
heart to you."

She felt again the humiliation of her transparent feelings and ducked her head to hide the pain. "I'm sorry I
put you in such an untenable position."

Flynn put his hand under her chin and lifted her face to
look at him. "Sorry?" He sounded incredulous. "You're
apologizing for loving me?"

She blinked. "Surely that's the least I can do. My silly
infatuation was not only embarrassing to you, but kept
you from the woman you wanted."

"Infatuation!" He removed his hand from her chin.
"Are you telling me that it was just infatuation you felt
for me in Central America, and after we were married?"

She forced herself to continue looking at him. "Of
course. What else could it have been?" She paused for a
moment, half expecting to be struck dead for telling such
a deliberate lie. "I was too young and unworldly to know
the difference between true love and a schoolgirl crush. It
wasn't until I was on my own that I realized how dependent I'd been all my life."

"I tried my best to take good care of you." He sounded
defensive, almost apologetic—as if his best hadn't been
good enough.

For some reason she was making things worse instead
of better, and she wanted to scream with frustration. She

couldn't bear for him to think that he'd failed her in any way.

Reaching out, she took his hand and cupped it against her cheek. "You took such good care of me that I never bothered to grow up," she said, trying to keep the yearning that welled inside her out of her voice. "Being cloistered is a safe and peaceful way to live, and I needed that in the beginning of our marriage. But over a period of time it sapped my ability to survive on my own. When I realized that you'd only stayed married to me out of a sense of obligation, it nearly destroyed me."

Flynn swore lustily, something he almost never did, and pulled away from her as he got to his feet. "Why won't you believe me when I tell you I didn't want a divorce?"

Mary Beth sighed. "Because I saw you kissing Vanessa, and it wasn't a platonic embrace."

He ran his hand through his hair and let out his breath. "All right, I behaved like a jerk. I've never denied that, but one kiss doesn't constitute adultery. If you hadn't run away, we could have worked things out."

She was aware of the other people in the room, and the fact that this discussion should be held in private. It was time to draw it to a close and leave.

She stood also. "Maybe we could have, Flynn," she said wearily, "but it would never have worked for long. Actually, you did me a favor by being indiscreet. Sort of like throwing the baby in the water to force it to swim. It was the only way I'd ever have gone out on my own and learned to survive without someone taking care of me. I like the feeling, and I'll never again be dependent on a man."

Before anyone else could speak, she picked up her purse and started for the desk. "Now, I really must be going. If I may use your phone, I'll just call a cab."

Flynn caught her by the arm. "I'll take you home," he said, and his tone brooked no argument.

Half an hour later they were finally cruising down the freeway in Flynn's BMW. It had taken Mary Beth quite a while to say goodbye to Flynn's mother and sisters. She'd learned that Joan was returning to Baltimore with her daughters in a few days, and it was unlikely she'd be seeing any of them again.

Sinking back into the leather upholstery, Mary Beth sighed. "I'm glad I came to the service today. I feel better now after seeing all of you again. I only wish Edward..." Her throat tightened. "I loved him very much."

Flynn glanced at her. "Then my father was a lucky man, since you're apparently more inclined toward infatuation than loving." He sounded angry.

She blinked with surprise. Was Flynn upset because she'd denied loving him? But why? What did he want from her, for heaven's sake? Blind adoration?

Well, he'd had that, too, but she wasn't going to admit it. "Loving hurts," she said simply. "Everyone I've loved has left me."

Now it was Flynn who looked surprised. "What do you mean?"

She shrugged. "First Dad and Mother, now Edward."

"But they died."

"So who said I have to be rational? They still left me behind to grieve. I don't think I want to love anymore."

For a moment he didn't respond, then he asked, "What about Donald MacGregor? Are you in love with him?"

Don. She'd forgotten all about him. Maybe that was her curse. Was she forever destined to compare every man she met with Flynn Warren?

It didn't make sense. Flynn was no saint. He'd betrayed her. Maybe not the ultimate betrayal of adultery, but he'd stayed married to her under false pretenses when he had wanted another woman. His marriage to her had been a sham, and that was the worst betrayal of all.

"Maybe I am in love with Don," she said, making her statement sound as convincing as she could. "He's a nice man. He'd be a good husband, and I want children."

"You'd get married just to have children?" He sounded incredulous.

"Why not? You were never in love with me, but still you stayed married to me for four years...." A sign above the freeway caught her eye. "Oh, take the next turnoff to get to my place."

For several minutes their attention was focused on her guiding him through a maze of streets until they reached the unpretentious neighborhood where she lived. For the first time she realized just how second-class it really was, probably because she was seeing it from Flynn's viewpoint.

As they rounded a corner, she pointed to a rambling Spanish-style stucco two-story building at the end of the block. "There it is," she said. "You can turn in at the driveway."

The complex was built in a square around a courtyard and parking area. The red tile roof was still bright, but the stucco was chipped and stained and in need of a whitewash.

He followed her instructions and drove into the small neglected courtyard. Again Mary Beth was aware of the unkempt grass and the faded plastic upholstered lounge chairs. The one saving grace was the magnificent old pepper tree that shaded the whole area.

Flynn parked in a spot marked Guest and looked around. "Is this where you live?" He didn't attempt to hide his disdain.

She immediately bristled. "It may have escaped your notice, Dr. Warren, but not everyone can afford to live on a cliff overlooking the celebrated shoreline of La Jolla."

He looked at her and frowned. "Don't be sarcastic, it doesn't become you."

She felt like a child being reprimanded, and she didn't like it a bit. "Then quit being so snobbish," she retorted. "Remember, I didn't invite you here. If it offends your sensibilities, you're free to leave."

He didn't deign to answer, but followed her up the outside staircase and along the wraparound balcony until they came to her front door, which faced the driveway.

She unlocked it, then turned to face him. "Thank you for bringing me home—"

"I'd like to come in," he interrupted.

"But..." She couldn't very well refuse, even though she didn't want him to see her shabby little apartment. On the other hand she had nothing to be ashamed of. It was clean and neat and comfortable.

"All right," she said, and opened the door directly into the living room.

He followed her in and looked around. She and Peggy rented the place furnished, and it had the look of an aging showroom display. Everything matched, but the effect was uninspired and impersonal.

"Sit down," she said, "and I'll get us something to drink. Do you still like Virgin Marys?"

He grinned. "You remembered. Yes, that'll be fine. Are you still sipping Shirley Temples?"

She grinned back. "You bet. Keeps my head clear and my driving record free of DUIs."

Several minutes later she emerged from the kitchen and handed Flynn his spiced tomato juice, then sat down in the chair across from him with her concoction of fruit juices and ginger ale.

He took a sip of his drink, then cleared his throat. "Are you having trouble making ends meet financially, Mary Beth?"

She tensed. "Of course not," she said indignantly. "I'm doing just fine."

"Then why are you living here? What are they paying teachers these days? Surely you can do better than this."

What right did he have to inquire into her finances? "Don't judge other people's living conditions by yours, Flynn." Her tone was abrupt. "You were born into wealth, and except for the few months you spent as a medical missionary in Central America, you've never known anything else. On the other hand I lived amongst poverty all my life until I married you."

She looked around her and was content with what she saw. "What do you have against my apartment? It's clean and warm and dry, which is more than I can say for the shack I grew up in.

"I like living here with Peggy. Our neighbors are wonderful people. Mrs. Jacinto, the elderly widow next door, brings us gazpacho and home-baked cookies. Max, the middle-aged bachelor in 3D, is always available to take care of any plumbing, electrical or automobile emergencies, and the Munoz family in 1A named their new baby Mary Elizabeth after me because I help their eldest son with his homework. Besides, it's close to the school where we teach."

Flynn looked shocked. "You mean you work in this area?"

She wondered why she hadn't noticed this condescending side of him before. Probably because she hadn't seen it. Not only had she been blinded by the stars in her eyes, but in his own rarified environment the subject would never have come up.

"Not exactly," she answered. "This is the classier part of the barrio. Peg and I teach in the slum."

He slammed his glass down on the coffee table. "Why do you insist on mocking me? I'm sorry if my concern for you is offensive, but I think I'm entitled to some straight answers. You're still my responsibility."

Her simmering anger flared into rage, and she jumped out of her chair. "I'm *not* your responsibility," she said from between clenched jaws. "I haven't been for three years, and I never will be again. And I *am* giving you straight answers. If you don't believe me, then come and see for yourself."

She grabbed up her purse and rummaged in it until she found her keys. "We'll take my car. Where we're going your fancy BMW would be stripped while you were still sitting in it."

Flynn tried to protest, but she strode out the door and he had no choice but to follow her. She led him to the Nissan and slid behind the wheel before he could insist on driving. He seemed more dumbfounded than angry, and she realized that she'd never openly defied him before. Well, he was going to find that his little pussycat had grown claws and learned to spit.

Chapter Four

The farther away from the apartment house they drove, the more run-down the neighborhoods became. By the time she parked in front of the school, Mary Beth could tell from his expression that Flynn no longer thought she was exaggerating when she called the area a slum.

"Well, here we are," she said cheerfully. "El Dorado elementary, one of the city's forgotten schools. Actually the curriculum is adequate and the staff is good, but the buildings, grounds and neighborhood leave a lot to be desired. Classes are out for the day and the place is all locked up, so I can't take you on a tour of the buildings, but we can drive around the corner and see the playground and the portable bungalows."

She slowly rounded the block and stopped again. A high chain link fence surrounded the property, but its neglected condition was clearly visible from the street. "Are all those bungalows classrooms?" Flynn asked.

"Yeah. The school was built in the thirties to accommodate about a third as many students as are now enrolled. The portables aren't bad, actually, except that the kids have to get out in the fog and rain to go from one to the other, or to the main building. We don't have a cafeteria, so the students have to eat their sack lunches in an all-purpose room. Those who didn't lose them or have them stolen on the way to school, that is."

"Why isn't there a cafeteria?" He sounded incredulous.

Mary Beth settled more comfortably in the seat. "When it was built, it was a neighborhood school and there was no need for one. The kids went home for lunch. Now we draw from a much larger area, but the excuse for not building one is lack of funds. Unfortunately, the parents just don't have enough clout to insist."

She looked around and spied another item of interest. Her intuition warned her not to call it to his attention, but she couldn't resist digging into his smug shell even further.

"Do you see that gray house across the street and about halfway down the block? The one that's all boarded up?"

Flynn nodded.

"That's our latest landmark. It was a crack house before the police raided it."

"Drugs!"

"Yep. Cocaine. It was after the raid that the school board closed the campus and won't allow any of the students to leave until their classes are over or an authorized person picks them up. Also all visitors have to clear the principal's office and get a pass before they can get in."

He looked appalled but said nothing as she drove home. Mary Beth was uneasy. She'd expected him to rant and rage, and his silence was unnerving.

When they got back to the apartment house, he slid out of the car and reached into his breast pocket. Extracting a slim leather case, he withdrew a business card and a gold pen. He turned the card over and wrote something on the back, then handed it to Mary Beth.

"That's my office address and phone number," he said. "My home address and number is on the back. If I can't be reached at either place, the exchange will answer and take a message. Call me anytime you need me."

He turned away and walked rapidly toward his BMW, leaving her staring after him, stunned and incredulous.

Flynn drove out of the courtyard without looking in Mary Beth's direction. He knew if he did, he'd either yell at her for being an idiot or kidnap her to keep her safe. Either action would earn him the back of her hand or a tongue-lashing, or both.

He could feel drops of sweat running down his body underneath his clothes, and he swallowed down the bile that threatened to rise as another wave of nausea swept over him. Pulling over to the curb, he shut off the engine and slumped across the steering wheel.

Without a doubt this had been the most horrendous day of his life. Even surpassing the massacre at the mission, or Mary Beth's sudden disappearance. At those times he'd had too much to do to notice the toll the events were taking on his stamina, but today he'd been battered with a series of bone-jarring emotions from the time he got out of bed after a restless night.

It would have been bad enough just getting through the last week of his father's life and the memorial service, but being hit with the shock of seeing Mary Beth again plus her startling revelations was overpowering.

Mary Beth. The relief of knowing she was all right and once more within his reach was almost as debilitating as the grief he felt at losing his father.

She'd changed drastically in the past three years. No longer the cuddly child-wife he'd nurtured and protected, but a self-confident teacher who'd learned to live a full and satisfying life without him. She no longer either needed or wanted his love.

He banged the steering wheel with his fist. Well, what had he expected? Any man who had been too blind and stupid to realize what a treasure she was didn't deserve her.

The tragedy of it was that he had known but messed up anyway. They hadn't been married more than two weeks before he began wanting her. He told himself it was just the normal reaction of a healthy male toward an appealing young woman who was legally bound to him.

That rationalization hadn't helped a bit, and as time went on, the wanting turned to desire, and the desire to need, until it was all he could do to control himself. Even though he could hardly bear to have her out of his sight, he still hadn't recognized his feelings as love. He'd told himself that he was just taking care of her, temporarily providing her with a home and education until she was prepared to be on her own.

When he finally couldn't hold out any longer and consummated the marriage, he'd been in for another shock. Instead of just the release of pent-up lust that he'd expected, it had been an almost mystical experience of such magnitude that he'd been deeply shaken.

Flynn shifted uncomfortably and realized that his thoughts had aroused him. Damn! He sat up and started the engine. He had all he could endure without that. Easing the car into traffic, he headed for the freeway.

Maybe Mary Beth didn't need him any longer, but he sure as hell needed her. No way was he going to let her get away from him a second time. She still had some feelings for him. He'd felt her response when he'd held her in his arms. The warmth and the electricity were still there, but this time he would take it slow.

It occurred to him that he'd never courted her. One day she'd been the teenager with a crush on the Anglo doctor, and the next day she was his wife and later his lover.

He'd cheated her out of the most important part of the mating game, the preliminary dance of the lovers. The dates, the long walks down the romantic byways, the hours of just talking and getting to know each other. He'd never asked her what her goals were, her dreams for the future, her thoughts about a family.

The freeway ramp loomed ahead, and he turned onto it. What a self-centered lout he'd been! It was no wonder she'd walked out on him and gotten as far away as she could

Still, something had guided her back to him. That in itself was a miracle. For some reason he was being given a second chance, and this time he was going to do it right!

Shortly after lunch on Saturday afternoon, Mary Beth was out in the community laundry room transferring the washed clothes and linens into a dryer. She hadn't heard from Flynn since he'd left so abruptly on Wednesday afternoon, and the strain was rubbing her nerves raw. Her tumultuous thoughts were suddenly interrupted when Peggy, dressed like Mary Beth in old jeans and a sweatshirt, came through the door.

"There's a phone call for you," she said. "It's Flynn."

Mary Beth froze. "Are you sure?"

Peggy nodded. "Yes. I asked him if I could tell you who was calling, and he said, 'Tell her it's Flynn.'"

Mary Beth dropped the towel she was holding into the basket and started out of the room, but Peggy caught her by the arm and detained her. "Look, Mary Beth, I know it's none of my business, but are you sure you want to get involved with your ex-husband again?"

"What do you mean by 'involved'?" Mary Beth asked testily. She'd told her roommate about meeting Flynn and his family at the memorial service and later spending the day with them, but that didn't give her the right to interfere.

"You know what I mean. This man hurt you badly once, are you going to give him a second crack at you? At least take it slowly. Give yourself time to get to know him without the hero worship clouding your judgment."

Mary Beth stiffened. "Now look, I—"

"I know," Peggy said, and released her friend's arm. "I'm interfering and you don't like it. I don't blame you, but I've seen the effect of those nightmares you have. I'm only saying don't be too quick to trust the man who's responsible for them. Just because he didn't marry the woman he was interested in doesn't mean he hasn't had others since."

Mary Beth knew Peggy was right, but she was annoyed all the same and merely nodded as she walked away.

Hurrying into the apartment, she reached the kitchen, then stopped for a moment to catch her breath. She wasn't going to let Flynn know how anxiously she'd been waiting to hear from him.

"Hello, Flynn," she said, and hoped she sounded friendly but a little distant.

"Hello, sweetheart," he said softly, and her knees buckled as she leaned against the wall for support. "Did I call at a bad time?"

She hadn't heard his voice on the phone in years, but it still had the power to send prickles down her backbone. Especially when he called her 'sweetheart.'"

"Oh, no...no, I was just over in the laundry room. How are you? You left so abruptly the other day. Were you angry with me?" She held her breath, hoping he wouldn't berate her about where she worked.

"Not angry, just upset," he said. "It had been a grueling day, and I wasn't feeling very well. I'm sorry if I was rude. Will you let me make it up to you by taking you to brunch at the Hotel Del Coronado tomorrow morning?"

Brunch at the Del Coronado! What woman wouldn't want to have Sunday brunch at the last of the extravagantly conceived seaside hotels with the man she loved? Especially if they'd spent the night before in one of the large luxurious rooms under the round red gabled roof.

Good grief, what happened to that "friendly distance" she'd intended to keep? Mary Beth quickly reined in her runaway imagination and tried to compose herself. "I'd love to. Will eleven o'clock be all right?"

He agreed and they talked for a few minutes, but then his call-waiting signaled an incoming call and he had to hang up.

Later that afternoon Peggy had gone grocery shopping and Mary Beth was cleaning out the refrigerator when the doorbell rang. Drying her hands on a towel, she answered it to find George, the apartment-house manager, and a brawny middle-aged man facing her.

"Sorry to bother you, Ms. Warren," George said pleasantly, "but I want to introduce your new neighbor,

Mr. Sullivan, who's just moved into the apartment next door.''

The other man reached out his hand and smiled. "Hi. Harry's the name.''

She took his hand and smiled in return. "I'm Mary Beth Warren. Welcome to the neighborhood.''

"Harry here's got a problem, an' I told him you and Ms. MacGregor might be able to help him out,'' George said.

Harry reached into his pocket and brought out a wallet, then extracted two cards and handed them to her. "I'm a security guard. Here's my guard card. Could we talk to you for a few minutes?''

She examined the card. It had a recent picture of the man and a description that told her he was fifty-one years old, six feet tall and weighed two hundred twenty-five pounds.

"Yes, I suppose so," she said, torn between being neighborly and being cautious. Still, she was well acquainted with George and knew he'd have checked out his new tenant before introducing him to her. "Would you come in?''

It was still raining and decidedly chilly, and they thanked her and entered the living room.

When they were seated, Harry spoke. "I think you'll agree that this is a real coincidence,'' he began. "I'm starting a new job Monday as security officer for the El Dorado Elementary School, and I understand that you and Ms. MacGregor teach there.''

"Yes, we do," Mary Beth admitted. "Are you replacing Bill?''

He shook his head. "No, just supplementing him. The thing is that my truck conked out on me today and I had to have it towed to the garage. They won't even look at it until Monday, and then who knows how long it will take to fix it. Meanwhile, I'm without wheels. Could I catch a ride with you two for a few days? Naturally I'll pay my share of the expenses."

She'd been covertly watching him, and he seemed open and friendly. A big man with black hair streaked with gray, dark brown eyes and muscles that rippled under his plaid flannel shirt, he appeared to be exactly what he said he was.

"We'd be happy to have you ride with us," she said. "Peggy and I leave here no later than seven-thirty in the mornings, and usually leave school between three-thirty and four in the afternoons. Does that fit with your schedule?"

"Great," he said, and stood up. "Thanks, I really appreciate this. See you early Monday morning."

The next morning, Sunday, Mary Beth took a long time choosing an outfit to wear. She finally decided on a magenta wool dress with long sleeves and a plain round neckline. With it she wore a large scarf in a matching shade of magenta, featuring a bold leaf print in white, fawn and teal. The color was flattering and brought out the natural rosiness of her cheeks; her only makeup was lipstick and a touch of brown mascara and eyebrow pencil.

She let her blond hair fall loose around her shoulders, knowing it was a mistake but unable to resist. Flynn had always preferred it that way, and her vanity demanded that she remind him she could be sexy and seductive even though it was important that she impress on her overprotective ex-husband that she was an independent career-oriented woman.

A few hours later, Mary Beth had been home from church only a short while when Flynn arrived. For a moment they stood in the doorway just looking at each other, then he stepped inside and reached out his hands to run them down the long length of her hair.

"Now you look like my sweet young wife," he murmured huskily, and took her in his arms.

For a long time they stood there holding each other as she drank in the heady scent of his expensive cologne and the touch of his smooth cheek against her own. Her guard lowered, and a peaceful feeling of warmth and happiness welled inside her as he cuddled her against him and let the silence envelop them.

After a while he traced her spine to the small of her back, then splayed his fingers across the rise of her buttocks. "So much for all my good intentions," he murmured wryly against her ear. "I was determined not to touch you today except in a brotherly manner."

Mary Beth's heart pounded as she caressed his nape. "You haven't done anything too unbrotherly so far," she whispered.

"That's only because I have a tight rein on my limited self-control, but it's not going to last much longer if I don't put you away from me." His tone betrayed his strain.

It occurred to her that all she had to do was kiss the sensitive spot at the side of his throat and move against him to shatter that limited control. He'd always responded to her with passion, but that was no longer enough. She needed his love, too. Now that she knew she'd never had that love, the passion, although always shattering in its intensity, would be empty and meaningless.

It took all her strength to move reluctantly away from him, but he didn't try to stop her. "I . . . I guess we'd better be leaving," she said shakily. "You probably have reservations."

"Yes, I do." He took her arm in a most brotherly manner and escorted her to the car.

Riding in Flynn's BMW was like floating on air, and Mary Beth sank back into the seat and relaxed. "How's your mother?" she asked. "Have she and your sisters gone back to Baltimore yet?"

"Yes," Flynn answered. "They left Friday morning. Mom's all right physically, but emotionally she's shattered. She and Dad had been married for almost forty-five years and they relied on each other totally."

Mary Beth could empathize strongly with her ex-mother-in-law's grief. She suspected that it wouldn't be much different than the way she'd felt when she'd lost Flynn, even though he had not died.

"I'm so sorry," she said, "but at least she has you and your sisters. Is she going to live back there now?"

"She doesn't plan to, but she's not making any permanent decisions for the time being."

As they approached the spectacular two-mile-long bridge that linked the Coronado peninsula with downtown San Diego, Mary Beth's excitement mounted. In all the months she'd lived here, she'd never been to the century-old historical monument that was one of the city's most outstanding attractions. She sat forward in the seat, trying to see everything while they were still high above the water.

Flynn glanced at her. "What's the matter? Don't you like high bridges?"

"I love them," she said happily. "I've wanted to cross this one ever since I came here."

"You mean you've never been to the Del Coronado before?"

"Never. I've heard so much about their fabulous Sunday brunches, but I didn't like to come alone."

"What about your 'dear friend' Don? Couldn't you get him to bring you?"

The sarcasm that always tinged his voice when he mentioned Don was back.

"He never suggested it and I wouldn't ask him," she answered. "It's awfully expensive."

Flynn had a pensive expression as he reached over and took her hand. "Well, I can afford it, and I'll bring you here every Sunday if it will always please you this much." He squeezed her hand. "Sometime soon we're going to have to talk about finances, honey."

Too late she realized that she should never have mentioned money. What she thought of as expensive was average for him, and he seemed determined to upgrade her standard of living.

Reluctantly she pulled her hand away and folded it with the other one in her lap. "No, we aren't going to discuss finances, Flynn. I'm happy with things just the way they are."

"I'm not," he said, and captured her hand again. "Don't pull away from me, Mary Beth. I'm sorry if my concern for you is offensive, but you're very dear to me."

His words and the tone he used brought a lump to her throat, and her lips trembled as she rubbed her cheek against his arm. The fine wool of his gold blazer was warm against her skin.

"Not offensive, don't ever think that. You're very dear to me, too, and I don't want to be a burden."

He started to protest, and she hurried on. "No, wait, I'm not expressing myself well. I realize that you'd probably be willing to support me for the rest of my life, but I can't allow that and still keep my self-respect. I won't be any more beholden to you than I already am. I need to be independent, otherwise I'm nothing but an extension of you."

"You *are* an extension of me, Mary Beth, no matter how independent you become, just as I'm an extension of you. Our problem is that we can't both grasp that fact at the same time."

She started to say something, but he put his finger to her lips. It was only then that she realized they were off the bridge and stopped at a red light on the Coronado peninsula.

"I know you don't understand what I'm talking about," he continued, "but someday you will. Meanwhile I'll continue to be possessive, and you'll fight me every step of the way. Now, we're only a couple of blocks from the hotel, so let's not quarrel. I want your first brunch at the Del Coronado to be a very special occasion."

The light turned to green, and a couple of minutes later they drove into the hotel parking lot.

To Mary Beth's enthusiastic gaze, the Hotel Del Coronado was every bit as fabulous as she'd been led to believe. Although greatly enlarged since its grand opening in 1888, the original round building with its turrets, tall cupolas, hand-carved wooden pillars and Victorian gingerbread still stood as a monument to the past.

Inside she gasped at the luxury of thick maroon carpeting, dark hardwood pillars, paneling and balcony balustrade and, most spectacular of all, the magnificent crystal chandeliers.

They walked through the crowded lobby to the desk, where Flynn bought their brunch tickets then ushered her into the palatial Crown room. A hostess seated them at a table by the windows that overlooked a colorful garden. She then explained that they were to serve themselves from the buffet tables that spanned the middle of the huge rectangular room.

"And don't forget dessert," she concluded. "There's a dessert table for each side, and they're marked with balloons. Yours is over there." She pointed, and Mary Beth spotted the bouquet of colorful balloons hovering above the tempting array of sweets.

A waitress appeared almost immediately after the hostess left, and poured sparkling champagne into the stemmed crystal glass at each place setting. Mary Beth grinned and picked hers up. "I'm not fond of champagne, but since this is a special occasion I'd better drink it."

"Definitely," Flynn said, and touched his glass to hers. "It can't be a special occasion without the bubbly."

They both took a sip, and she let her fascinated gaze roam around their end of the room. Various sizes of tables covered with pink linen cloths and set with red linen napkins, crystal glasses and heavy ornate silver flatware filled all the available space without seeming to crowd.

Her glance wandered to the ceiling, and a little cry of surprise escaped her. "Oh, look, Flynn. The chandeliers are shaped like crowns!"

He smiled, obviously enjoying her delight. "I know, and notice the unique arched ceiling. It's constructed of natural finished sugarpine and fitted together entirely with wooden pegs. It's recognized as one of the architectural and engineering masterpieces of the world. Now, I don't know about you, but I didn't have breakfast this morning and I'm starved. Shall we go get something to eat?"

As they approached the buffet tables, Mary Beth noticed that the other side of the room was also filled with diners. She estimated that the Crown room must seat close to a thousand people.

The first table featured breakfast foods. She helped herself to scrambled eggs, ham, a slice of melon, and when she couldn't decide between a Danish roll and a slice of nut bread, she consulted Flynn, who advised, "Take one of each. You can worry about your weight tomorrow."

She chuckled as he took some of everything, including the eggs Benedict, fruit juice and hot cereal with cream. "I gather you're going to diet tomorrow, too?" she teased.

His eyes twinkled. "Never have to," he bragged. "I use it all up running around the hospital corridors."

At the second table they added cold cuts, cheeses, a vast array of salads and an assortment of breads and rolls, only to discover that there was no room on their plates for even a taste of the fragrant hot dishes bubbling lightly over small butane flames on the third table.

"I need another platter and two more hands," Mary Beth wailed.

Flynn eyed her overflowing plate and laughed. "Honey, if you manage to put away all that, you can come back for more."

When they were seated again at their table, a waitress came with coffee. "Does it live up to your expectations?" Flynn asked.

"Oh, yes." She knew she was behaving like a child in a toy store, but she couldn't help it. It was a wonderful experience and she was enjoying every minute of it.

"The food is delicious," she continued. "You're going to spoil me for cold cereal and half-burned toast."

He looked at her with his expressive brown eyes. "And why is your morning toast half-burned?"

She grinned. "I see I'm going to have to confess my secret. That expensive education you so generously provided me with was deficient in one area; I'm a lousy cook."

Flynn laughed again, and it was a lovely sound. "Remind me to get a refund from good old University of Maryland." His gaze roamed inquiringly over her. "You don't look undernourished; how have you managed the past three years?"

"In Madrid I bought hot lunches at school and snacked at night," she explained. "Then, when I came to San Diego and moved in with Peggy, we took turns cooking, but after a few of my meals she tactfully suggested that she do the cooking and I the cleaning up."

He put his hand over hers on the table. "I'd better take you home with me and have Lars teach you to cook."

Take her home with him! The very sound of the phrase made her burn with yearning. She'd been so happy living with Flynn in blissful ignorance of his true feelings. If only she'd never found out about Vanessa!

No, she didn't mean that. It was always better to face reality than to live a fantasy. At least that was what she wanted to believe.

Anxiously she dragged her runaway thoughts back to the subject at hand. "Who's Lars?" she asked.

"Lars is a retired wrestler who works for me as sort of a jack-of-all-trades. I suppose if given a title it would have to be male housekeeper. He keeps the house clean, does the yard work, fixes everything that has to be fixed and could rival any chef in town with his cooking."

Laughter bubbled from deep inside her. "He sounds like just the man I need. Is he by any chance looking for a wife?"

Flynn's expression immediately hardened. "If he is he can look somewhere else," he said in a dangerously cool tone. "You belong to me."

Mary Beth opened her mouth to blast him, when he quickly held up his arms in a defensive gesture. "Sorry, I apologize," he said hastily. "I knew that was the wrong thing to say the second it was out. You don't belong to me. Intellectually I know that, but . . ."

He put down his arms and again took her hand. "When we said our marriage vows, I agreed to love and cherish you, to care for you in sickness and in health until death parted us. I took that vow seriously. I cherished you, took care of you—"

"But you didn't love me." The words had a strangled sound as tears welled in her blue eyes.

"I did love you," he said desperately as his hand tightened on hers.

"Then why were you kissing Vanessa?" With her other hand she dabbed at her eyes.

Flynn slumped back in his chair. "It always comes back to that, doesn't it? Other married men have affairs with their secretary or the woman next door and are forgiven, but I kissed my ex-fiancée once and get consigned to purgatory."

"It's not like that and you know it," she said, keeping her voice low. She finished drying her eyes and put the napkin down. "Tell me, Flynn. If it had been the other way around, if you'd caught me kissing another man, what would you have done?"

He raised his face and looked directly at her. "I'd have killed him."

Mary Beth shook her head sadly. "No, you're not a violent man, but I suspect you would have wanted to because your masculinity would have been threatened. No man wants to think that he can't satisfy his woman, but it works the same way with women. Do you think my femininity wasn't threatened?"

Her features twisted into a grimace. "It was not only threatened, it was demolished. To suddenly be confronted with the fact that all the time we were married you'd been in love with another woman destroyed me. You had no right to keep that to yourself. You should have at least told me in the beginning what the situation was and let me decide whether or not I wanted to live with you under those conditions."

"I couldn't do that, you'd have left me," he said in a tone that sounded reasonable even though what he said didn't make any sense. Why hadn't he wanted her to leave him if he'd been in love with Vanessa?

"You're right, I would have," she answered, trying to keep her own voice from breaking, "and I should have been allowed to make that decision. Don't tell me that all you're guilty of is a stolen kiss with an ex-fiancée. Our whole marriage was based on a lie!"

Flynn started to interrupt, but she wouldn't let him. "Oh, I know, you never told me you loved me. Did you think I wasn't aware of that? Well, I was, but I was also appallingly unsophisticated in those days. I thought you were just shy about putting your feelings into words."

She picked up the sparkling crystal champagne glass and finished what was left of its contents. "My naïveté doesn't excuse you, Flynn. You lied indirectly by allowing me to think you wanted to be married to me. I don't doubt but that you did it out of kindness, but it was still a form of manipulation. That's what I find hard to forgive.

"I should have been consulted about a situation so vitally important to my own future. It would have been a lot easier to take at that time than it was after sharing four years of lovemaking with you."

Chapter Five

Flynn cringed as though Mary Beth had hit him. "There's just enough truth in what you believe to make it difficult to deny," he said huskily, "but you've got it all wrong, love. We can't argue such a complicated misconception here, there's neither the time nor the privacy, but I promise you we will get it straightened out and soon."

His eyes were pleading with her for understanding. "Let's not quarrel anymore. I had such hopes that today would be a happy one. Can we call a truce and pretend that we're courting?"

The corners of her mouth quivered into a half smile. "Courting?"

He grinned. "I'm an old-fashioned guy. I want to court the lovely lady who's captured my fancy."

Her smile widened. "Fancy?" She stifled a giggle.

He picked up her hand and kissed it. "If I said you'd captured my heart, you wouldn't believe it, so we'll settle on 'fancy' for now." He pushed back his chair and stood. "Come on, we still have to tackle the hot dishes and desserts."

An hour later they'd finally taken the last bite of chocolate torte, strawberry cheesecake and several other samples of the rich and luscious array of sweets while they lingered over coffee.

Mary Beth leaned back and put her hand on her stomach. "Darn it, Flynn," she said grumpily, "you're a doctor. You shouldn't have let me eat those desserts. You know what a glutton I am."

He eyed her fondly. "Overdosing on chocolate and sugar once a year won't affect your health, but if I were a dentist I'd be very cross with you."

She made a face at him. "Oh, yeah? What about all that goo you ate?"

He leaned over and pressed his finger to the tip of her nose. "I enjoyed it very much, thank you. Now if you think you can waddle out of here, how would you like to go downstairs and take in the shops?"

Her eyes widened. "Shops?"

He laughed. "I knew that would get your attention. The bottom level is a shopper's paradise of boutiques. Are you interested?"

She picked up her purse and stood. "Just lead me to them," she said happily.

Flynn did lead her down a flight of stairs to a floor that also opened out onto ground level on the sloping terrain. The place was swarming with people, from businessmen and women in tailored suits to tourists in jeans and T-shirts.

Mary Beth and Flynn wandered hand in hand from one elegant shop to another while she exclaimed over the merchandise. "Oh, look," she said admiringly as she ran her hand carefully over a soft fluffy blue cashmere sweater. "Isn't it exquisite?"

He squeezed the hand he was holding. "Yes, it is. Will you let me buy it for you?"

She quickly moved on. "No. Thanks, Flynn, but no. I'm still wearing the clothes you bought me while we were married."

His gaze roamed over her. "I don't remember seeing that dress before."

She managed a smile. "Sure you have, but I used to wear it with jewelry instead of a scarf."

A cloud passed over his face. "You didn't take your jewelry when you left. I still have it in the safe-deposit box."

"It wasn't mine to take," she said carefully. "It belonged to your wife."

He tensed and drew in his breath. "Dammit, I bought the jewelry for *you*, not some impersonal title. Why are you being so stubborn—"

"Please, Flynn," she begged, pulling her hand from his, "lower your voice, we're attracting attention."

He looked around them. "All right," he said more quietly, "but we do need to talk. Let's go outside where we can have more privacy."

Mary Beth knew he was right. Until she could convince him that she was content with her life, he'd never give up on trying to take care of her.

They went through one of the glass doors and onto the terrace that overlooked the ocean. They found an empty table and sat down.

"Are you warm enough?" he asked anxiously. "The breeze off the water can be chilly."

"I'm fine," she answered. "This dress is wool."

For a while they sat looking out over the vast expanse of ocean. It was such a beautiful setting, Mary Beth thought. If only she and Flynn didn't rub angry sparks off each other every time they were together.

It didn't used to be that way. When they'd been married, they had never quarreled. Or rather Flynn had scolded and she had apologized. She hadn't realized how submissive she'd been until she'd lived on her own for three years.

It was no wonder they argued now. She had finally learned to think for herself and not let her husband tell her what she could and couldn't do. She doubted that Flynn would ever accept the fact that she was now his equal, not his responsibility.

He brought her attention back to him when he spoke. "Mary Beth, what did you live on from the time you dropped out of sight in Baltimore until you started collecting a paycheck? How did you get to Spain with no money? You didn't make any withdrawals from the account I'd opened for you. All you took from the house were your clothes and personal items."

She flinched as she realized how cruel she'd been to leave with no explanation. Her only defense was that she'd been too upset by the divorce action to understand that he'd worry about her.

"Don't forget I took the new Jaguar you'd given me," she explained. "I drove it to New York and sold it. It brought plenty of money for the flight to Madrid and living expenses until I got settled. I was never destitute. Surely you must have known that."

He scowled. "No, dammit, I didn't know that. It never occurred to me that you'd left the country. I thought you were using the car."

She looked away, unable to bear the anguish in his eyes. "I'm truly sorry. It was never my intention to worry you, but I can see now how selfish it was of me not to tell you my plans. It's just that I was so...so hurt, so humiliated, that all I could think of was getting away."

She heard him sigh. "Why didn't you at least take the money in your account? It was yours. There were no strings attached."

"I know," she said softly, "but I'd done nothing but take from you ever since my parents had been killed. I'd never been able to give you anything. I took the car and my clothes because I needed them, but I couldn't take all that money."

Flynn groaned and muttered an oath as he pushed his chair back with such force that it tipped over when he stood. He didn't look at her, but strode hurriedly off the terrace and down the slanting lush lawn to the beach.

Mary Beth watched as he reached the water's edge, then turned left and walked along it. She closed her eyes and let the fading warmth of the sun penetrate the chill of regret and apprehension.

Why was it that they couldn't be together more than a few minutes at a time without lashing out? What made them so vulnerable to each other? Flynn didn't love her, and, although she'd never stopped loving him, she could no longer tolerate his dictatorial attitude.

What gave them the power to hurt each other so deeply? She'd wanted to spare him pain, and he'd wanted to take care of her. Two commendable intentions, so why had they resulted in such torment?

When she opened her eyes again, Flynn was standing on the beach a block or so away, looking lonely and depressed, his shoulders slumped and his hands jammed into his pockets.

She couldn't sit there any longer. She was going to him whether he wanted her to or not.

Getting up, she walked across the terrace and the lawn, but when she got to the beach, she found it difficult walking on the loose sand in her high-heeled pumps. Finally she took them off and carried them as she trudged closer to the solitary figure of her ex-husband.

While she was still several yards away, he looked up and saw her approaching. For a second he just stood there watching her, then slowly he held out his arms. With a surge of joy Mary Beth threw down her shoes and ran into his embrace.

He held her close against him while she hugged him around his waist and buried her face in his chest. He rubbed his cheek in her hair, and for a long time they just stood there drawing strength from each other.

Finally it was Flynn who spoke. "I'm going to tell you something, sweetheart," he said huskily, "and I want you to listen and believe. You say you took but were never able to give while we were married. If you believe that, then it's no wonder you don't want anything more to do with me. I must have been a cold, unfeeling son of a..."

He paused, then continued without finishing the raw oath. "You gave me far more than I would ever have expected. You gave me warmth and loyalty and your trust, which I abused. You gave me laughter and beauty and contentment, which in turn made me feel so secure that I probably didn't bother to tell you how much it meant to me."

He ran his hands caressingly over her back. "You gave me your virginity, a precious gift, and when you got the hang of it, you gave me an intimacy that most men only dream of."

His arms tightened, and his lips sought the side of her throat. "You gave me love, and I gave you *things*. It was you who was cheated in our marriage. I was blessed a hundredfold and was too arrogant and stubborn to admit it until it was too late."

He released her, then cupped her face and lifted it so he could look into her eyes. "Don't ever again tell me what a sacrifice I made by marrying you. I was given a priceless gift and I threw it away."

Mary Beth was too choked with emotion to answer. Their gazes locked, and her mouth trembled as he slowly lowered his head. Their lips were almost touching when someone running by on the beach whistled and shouted encouragement, breaking the spell.

Flynn quickly raised his head and dropped his hands, then put an arm around her waist and led her back up the beach.

When they reached her shoes, he picked them up and looked at her feet. "Good heavens," he said with alarm. "Your feet are soaked and the breeze is chilly. Come on, let's get you out of those wet stockings before you catch cold."

They ran back to the hotel and around the outside of it to the parking lot. As soon as they were in the car, Flynn turned on the engine and the heater. By that time her cold feet had chilled her and she was shivering.

"Take off those panty hose," he said as he rummaged in the glove compartment and grabbed a disposable hand towel. "You won't get warm until you get dry."

Her eyes widened. "But I . . ." A sudden attack of shyness made her look away.

He stared at her with disbelief. "Oh, for heaven's sake, Mary Beth, I either watched you take them off or took them off you myself practically every day for four years.

Surely you're not going to have an attack of the vapors at the thought of removing them in my presence one more time.''

He sounded severe, but she caught the hint of amusement in his tone and giggled. "Vapors?"

He smiled and stroked one finger along her cheek. "My sweet little Victorian lady," he said softly. "I shouldn't tease you. It's a relief to know that you've retained your modesty after all this time. I'm just sorry you no longer feel comfortable enough to be uninhibited with me the way you used to be."

Her resistance melted, and she knew she'd take off all her clothes for him if he asked her to.

She leaned her face into his hand, and her lips parted as he continued to caress her. She wanted that kiss they'd come so near to sharing on the beach. They hadn't kissed since she'd caught him with Vanessa, but never in all that time had she stopped craving the feel of his mouth covering hers, his tongue stroking and probing, demanding the response that he'd taught her would make him moan with pleasure.

She knew he wanted it, too, she could see the need in his eyes, but after a moment he pulled back and opened the door. "I'm going to get a blanket out of the trunk," he said unsteadily, "and you'd better have those panty hose off by the time I get back or I'm going to strip them off you myself."

She was tempted to wait and let him remove them, but with a sad little sigh she acknowledged that neither of them was ready for that type of familiarity.

When he returned, she had already wadded the stockings up and set them on the dashboard. A twinge of disappointment flickered across his face as he got back into the car. "Put your legs in my lap," he said, and she swung around in her seat in order to do so.

Gently he dried her bare feet and brushed away the sand. His strong, smooth hands performing such an intimate task on her nude flesh sent tiny darts of desire straight up her legs and made her throb. She shifted restlessly, and in so doing her heel came in contact with the hardness that betrayed his own frustration.

He sucked in his breath and quickly wrapped the warm blanket around her feet and legs, then lifted them to the floor so she could turn around and sit up straight. Neither of them spoke as he started the engine and backed out of the parking space.

Once more they crossed the water on the long high bridge, and Mary Beth got a view of the San Diego skyline.

"It's almost six o'clock," Flynn said. "Would you like to go somewhere for dinner?"

She moaned in mock dismay. "I couldn't possibly eat another big meal, but I think I can round up something for sandwiches when we get back to the apartment if you'd like."

"I'd like," he said with a smile.

As they left the bridge and drove toward her address, Mary Beth started having second thoughts. What had she been thinking of, inviting Flynn to stay for supper? She was no longer so naive as to think they could control the flaming attraction that flared between them, if they were alone together in the privacy of one of their homes.

If he wanted to make love to her, she knew she wouldn't, couldn't resist, but she also knew that she could never survive that type of relationship with her self-respect intact. She'd been strictly brought up to believe that lovemaking was a beautiful part of marriage and not to be indulged in until the vows were spoken. She'd repeated those vows with Flynn once, and she'd intended them to be forever, but after the divorce, the law said they were no longer valid. Unfortunately, her conscience felt the same way.

Her gaze settled on his hands as they rested on the steering wheel. Strong, graceful hands with long fingers. The hands of a surgeon. The hands of a lover that had so many times aroused her with tender strokes, teasing strokes, urgent strokes, until she was mindless with need before he joined her in a rapture beyond bearing.

She was abruptly shaken out of her reverie when the car swerved into the courtyard of the apartment complex. She was relieved to see a light in her front window. Peggy was home!

Flynn parked and opened his door. "Don't take off the blanket," he said. "I'll come around and carry you."

"There's no need for that," she answered quickly. "I'm warm now, and my shoes aren't wet. I can walk."

When they got to her door, he held out his hand for her key, but she shook her head and rang the bell. "Peggy's home," she explained. "I always ring the bell to let her know I'm coming in, in case she has company."

"Does she do the same for you?" he asked brusquely.

Mary Beth shot him an annoyed look, but didn't answer when her roommate opened the door. They walked inside, and she introduced Flynn to Peggy.

Peggy looked him over appraisingly, then held out her hand. "I think I'd better warn you right now that if this relationship ever degenerates into a domestic clash, I'm on Mary Beth's side," she said in her usual brutally truthful manner.

He took her hand and locked gazes with her. "Good," he said. "So am I. Can we be friends?"

For a moment Peggy hesitated, then smiled. "Sure. I'm glad to meet you. I've been curious as hell."

He laughed. "So have I, and I'm happy to meet you, too."

It wasn't until then that Peggy noticed the panty hose in Mary Beth's hand. She raised one eyebrow inquiringly but said nothing, leaving Mary Beth to blush and stammer. "We—we went for a walk on the beach and I took off my shoes. The stockings got wet, see." Eagerly she showed Peggy the soaked stocking feet.

Peggy still didn't comment, which just flustered Mary Beth all the more. "If you'll both excuse me, I'll go change into something more comfortable...."

Good grief, she was just making it worse. Without another word she turned and hurried across the living room toward the hall and the bedrooms, with the sound of Flynn's laughter ringing in her ears.

Quickly she changed into maroon slacks and a matching sweater with heavy socks and white Reeboks.

The other two were in the kitchen fixing supper when she joined them. Flynn made coffee, Peggy fixed tuna sandwiches, and Mary Beth arranged a platter of raw vegetables and dip.

It was almost ten when Flynn looked at his watch and sighed. "Sorry, but I'm going to have to leave. I have a tonsillectomy scheduled for seven o'clock in the morning."

They all stood, and he took Mary Beth's arm and walked her toward the living room while Peggy started clearing the table.

At the door Flynn cupped Mary Beth's shoulders with his hands and looked at her. "I'm tied up until late at the hospital for the next two days, but will you have dinner with me on Wednesday?"

"I'm sorry, but I'm busy that night," she said regretfully.

He frowned. "Who with? Don?"

She tensed. "That's really none of your business, but yes, we're going out to dinner with another couple."

"Call him and tell him you can't go," he ordered in a tone that indicated he expected to be obeyed.

She glared at him. "Why? Because you say so? That doesn't work anymore, Flynn. I make my own choices, and I've no intention of breaking my date. If you want me to have dinner with you, it will have to be on a different night."

He drew in a breath as though he was going to upbraid her, then let it out again and turned away to open the door. "Never mind," he muttered, and walked out.

Mary Beth leaned unhappily against the closed door. This wasn't going to work at all. She and Flynn could never be lovers again. They couldn't even be friends. They weren't the same people now. At least she wasn't. All that was left of their previous relationship was the magnetic physical attraction that was no longer a pleasure but a torment.

Oh, what a tangled web we weave, when first we practice to deceive.

The quotation from Sir Walter Scott played over and over in Flynn's mind as he drove north, then west toward La Jolla. He probably hadn't thought of that rhythmic jingle since he was in college, but now he couldn't get it out of his mind.

The old boy knew what he was talking about, except that Flynn hadn't set out to deceive Mary Beth, it just evolved. Now he was hoisted on his own petard!

It wouldn't be so bad if he was sure she wasn't sleeping with Don MacGregor, but the uncertainty was eating him alive. If he knew her as well as he thought he did, then he had nothing to worry about. She was a firm believer in the standards their church taught, and that would prevent her from making love with any man who wasn't her husband.

But what if she'd changed? Three years was a long time to be on her own, and in a foreign country, too. Had some Romeo convinced her that her morals were old-fashioned and unsophisticated?

The sharp blade of suspicion turned painfully in his gut. Mary Beth was a highly sensual woman, and she treasured her newfound independence. Did that freedom include the right to sleep around if she felt the need?

If he really thought it did, he'd have told her everything that had happened since she'd disappeared when he'd learned that she was dating the other man.

He should have done so anyway, but he'd been too shocked and confused and grief-stricken that day of his father's funeral to make a coherent decision. Now he'd waited just long enough that she'd be doubly outraged. He was damned if he did and damned if he didn't, and the longer he waited the worse it got.

Still, he needed more time. Time to reestablish the bond that had once existed so strongly between them. Time to regain the trust she'd given so freely, and the love—or infatuation as she preferred to call it now—that she'd graced him with. Without those three things, he'd lose her forever when he confessed his latest sin, and that was a certainty.

The following morning Harry Sullivan was waiting at the car when Mary Beth and Peggy arrived to drive to school. Mary Beth introduced the new security guard to Peggy, who had heard about him but hadn't met him yet.

"Sure is nice of you ladies to let me share your car pool," he said as he got into the back.

Peggy turned in the front passenger seat so she could see him. "How come the school is putting on more security?" she asked. "Things have quieted down a lot around the neighborhood since they closed the crack house."

He shrugged. "I don't know. They called the agency and asked for another guard, so here I am."

Peggy was silent for a moment, then she spoke again. "It was quite a coincidence that you'd need a new apartment at the same time as you took a new job. Where'd you live before?"

Mary Beth listened as she drove, and she was surprised at the way Peggy probed into their new neighbor's life. When she'd told Peggy about him, her roommate had been unconvinced that giving a stranger a ride was wise. "I don't think it's a good idea," she'd said. "After all, we really don't know anything about him. It could be dangerous."

Mary Beth had assured her that the apartment manager had vouched for Harry, and that she, herself, had checked his credentials. "He's a nice, friendly guy," she'd assured Peggy. "Besides, if you can't trust a law officer, who can you trust?"

Peggy had looked at her with disbelief. "My God, girl, how did you manage to reach the ripe old age of twenty-four with all that innocence still untouched? Security guards aren't law officers. They don't even need any special schooling unless they want to carry a gun. Any person can apply, although I gather they do have to submit to a pretty thorough background check."

Finally Peggy had agreed, albeit grudgingly, that Harry Sullivan was probably the nice guy Mary Beth thought he was and withdrew her objection to letting him ride with them. Apparently, though, she was determined to find out more about him.

"I had an apartment in Escondido," he said in answer to Peggy's last question, mentioning a town just north of San Diego. "I moved because my landlord raised the rent and my ex-wife hit me up for more child support when our oldest daughter started college. Then I got this job clear down here on the coast, so I decided to move into a cheaper place and also save money on commuting."

Mary Beth was sure her ears were red with embarrassment. Harry had straightforwardly and without hesitation given them personal information that was really none of their business, and she was relieved when Peggy seemed satisfied and went on to another subject.

By the time her last class was over on Friday afternoon, Mary Beth was tired and discouraged. She hadn't heard from Flynn since his angry exit on Sunday, and although she'd told herself she wasn't going to go out with him again, she'd almost immediately started waiting for him to call.

She sighed and began cleaning off her desk. Her date with Don on Wednesday, the event that precipitated the quarrel with Flynn, had been a disappointment. She hadn't been able to keep her mind on the company she was with, and when Don kissed her at her door, it was all she could do not to push him away.

Darn Flynn! Why did he have to come back into her life, anyway? He was messing up all her carefully laid plans and playing havoc with her emotions.

Mary Beth had stepped into the closet to get her coat and purse when she heard someone come into the bungalow. Assuming it was Peggy coming by to see if she was ready to leave, she put on her coat and walked back into the room, then stopped.

It wasn't Peggy; it was Flynn standing there looking a little sheepish and totally endearing. Her heart speeded up, and it was all she could do to stay where she was and not throw herself into his arms. Was she never going to learn?

"Flynn," she said inanely, "what are you doing here?"

He took a few steps toward her, then hesitated. "I've come to ask for your help," he said. "I have a patient from this area who needs surgery, but his parents refuse to give their consent. They don't speak English, and they're afraid of the *gringo médico*. They seem to think I'm going to mutilate the child with a *daga*. My Spanish is good, but yours is excellent, and besides, you're a teacher. They'll trust you. You may even have taught some of their children. Will you go to their house with me to talk to them?"

"But the people around here can't afford to have you take care of their children," she blurted, then was immediately sorry when she saw his expression harden.

"How would you know that?" he asked icily. "I don't recall discussing my fee schedule with you."

She felt terrible. That was a cheap shot, but she hadn't intended it to be. She'd simply said the first thing that came into her mind, without realizing how it would sound.

She took a few steps closer so that they were within touching distance. "I'm sorry, Flynn," she said contritely. "I didn't mean that the way it sounded. It's just that the people around here live on the ragged edge of poverty, and they can't afford to consult doctors who practice in La Jolla."

His expression became colder. "What is it with you, Mary Beth? I don't remember your being such a reverse snob. What do you have against physicians charging fees for their services? This child was brought to the university hospital in critical condition, and since I'm damned good at what I do, I was called in. He needs surgery, but I can't operate without his parents' consent. I'll accept whatever Medical will pay me, and if the parents don't qualify for welfare, I'll do it for nothing."

Mary Beth couldn't remember ever feeling more ashamed. He was right, she had become a snob. Just because she was willing to work for less pay than she was qualified to demand, in order to help those less fortunate, it didn't make her a saint. Flynn had spent years of his life getting his education, and he was a gifted pediatrician. He was entitled to a lucrative practice.

She pressed her lips together to stop their quivering. "Flynn, you have to know that my respect for you is boundless. How could it be otherwise? When I first met you, you were serving as a medical missionary in the poorest section of Central America, treating all who came to you, without charge. If I sounded snobbish, I'm sorry, it was just a poor choice of words, but I've seen too many children go without medical care because, rightly or wrongly, their parents felt they couldn't afford it."

She sighed and looked away. "Of course I'll go with you, but we'll have to stop at my car first."

She started to walk past him, but in a surprise move he caught her to him. "Not so fast, love," he said huskily. "I need to hold you. It's been an eternity since Sunday."

She desperately needed to be held by him, and her willing body melted into his embrace.

"I'm sorry I barked at you," he murmured. "My nerves have been shot ever since you came back into my life. I want so badly for us to get along, but all I seem to do is make you happier to be rid of me. I spent all week trying to muster enough courage to get in touch with you and risk the very real possibility that you'd tell me to leave you alone."

She raised her face to his and asked the question that had been tormenting her. "Why haven't you kissed me, Flynn?"

With a strangled moan, he repositioned his arms under her lightweight coat and lowered his head to brush his lips against hers, then again, and again until she parted them and invited the intimacy he'd been seeking.

He tightened his arms around her, pulling her closer as his tongue probed for hers and joined it in a familiar caress that sent shivers through her. She closed her eyes and held him as she savored the deeply sensual contact that was Flynn's privilege exclusively.

With his large hands he roamed over her back, then settled them on the sides of her full breasts, making her gasp as pinpricks of flame spiraled to her core. A shudder gripped him, and he brusquely broke off the kiss and carefully pushed her away.

"That's why I haven't kissed you before," he said harshly. "We haven't had any privacy, and I knew my self-control wasn't up to a public encounter."

He took her arm and headed for the door. "Let's get out of here before I get us both arrested for indecency."

Chapter Six

Harry and Peggy were standing beside the car and talking as Flynn and Mary Beth approached. Mary Beth was certain she must look starry-eyed and thoroughly kissed, but there wasn't anything she could do about it except hope they wouldn't notice.

Flynn seemed to have regained his composure, but he'd always been able to hide his emotions better than she could. He hadn't been faking his passionate response to her, though. If only he loved her as much as he desired her!

The two by the car glanced up when they heard footsteps on the cement, and Peggy looked surprised to see Flynn. She said hello to him while Mary Beth introduced the two men. "Harry Sullivan, this is Dr. Flynn Warren. Harry is our new neighbor and car pool member," she explained, not bothering to mention that he was a security guard, since his uniform indicated that.

The men murmured greetings and shook hands, but Peggy looked puzzled. "I thought you two knew each other," she said. "I saw you talking together in the hallway of the main building."

Both men looked startled as she continued. "I didn't recognize you at the time, Flynn, because I didn't see your face, but that trench coat you're wearing is very distinctive. No one else around here wears anything near that expensive. It's a Burberry, isn't it?" she asked, mentioning the distinctive British label.

Flynn seemed to hesitate for a moment before answering. "Oh . . . yes. You probably did see us. I was asking Harry how to find Mary Beth's classroom, but we hadn't been introduced."

Harry nodded agreement and made a comment that Mary Beth didn't catch because she was too engrossed in wondering why Peggy seemed to attach so much importance to a chance meeting.

Opening her purse, she took out her car keys and held them out to her roommate. "I'm going with Flynn," she said, and explained where they were going and why. "You don't mind driving the car home, do you?"

Peggy took the keys. "Not at all. Harry and I'll find our way, but don't forget, I've got a date tonight, so if you want dinner you'll have to cook it. If you get home before I do, leave the outside light on. I'll be late."

As Mary Beth and Flynn drove away from the school in his BMW, she expected him to share Peggy's objection to allowing a stranger to carpool with them and scold her, but instead he talked about his patient. "The child's name is Roberto Garcia, and he's seven years old. Do you know him?"

She recognized the name. "Yes, he was in my class last semester."

WOW!

THE MOST GENEROUS
FREE OFFER EVER!
From the
Silhouette Reader Service™

ACCEPT FOUR BRAND NEW

YOURS

We'd like to send you four free Silhouette novels, worth $9.00, to introduce you to the benefits of the Silhouette Reader Service.™ We hope your free books will convince you to subscribe, but that's up to you. Accepting them places you under no obligation to buy anything, but we hope you'll want to continue your membership in the Reader Service.

So unless we hear from you, once a month we'll send you six additional Silhouette Romance™ novels to read and enjoy. If you choose to keep them, you'll pay just $2.25* per volume. And there is *no* charge for shipping and handling. There are *no* hidden extras! You may cancel at any time, for any reason, just by sending us a note or a shipping statement marked "cancel" or by returning any shipment of books to us at our cost. Either way the free books and gifts are yours to keep!

ALSO FREE!
ACRYLIC DIGITAL CLOCK/CALENDAR

As a free gift simply to thank you for accepting four free books we'll send you this stylish digital quartz clock — a handsome addition to any decor!

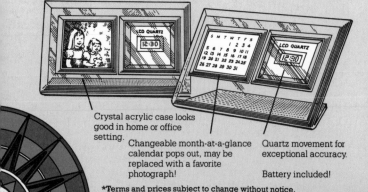

Crystal acrylic case looks good in home or office setting.

Changeable month-at-a-glance calendar pops out, may be replaced with a favorite photograph!

Quartz movement for exceptional accuracy.

Battery included!

*Terms and prices subject to change without notice.

Sales taxes applicable in NY and Iowa.

© 1990 HARLEQUIN ENTERPRISES LIMITE

SILHOUETTE ROMANCE™ NOVELS

FREE!

Silhouette Reader Service™

```
AFFIX
FOUR FREE BOOKS
STICKER HERE
```

YES, send me my four free books and gifts as
explained on the opposite page. I have affixed my
"free books" sticker above and my two "free gift"
stickers below. I understand that accepting these
books and gifts places me under no obligation ever to
buy any books; I may cancel at any time, for any
reason, and the free books and gifts will be mine to
keep!   215 CIS HAYG (U-S-R-01/90)

NAME _____
                        (PLEASE PRINT)

ADDRESS _____ APT. _____

CITY _____

STATE _____ ZIP _____

Offer limited to one per household and not valid to current Silhouette Romance™
subscribers. All orders subject to approval.

```
AFFIX FREE
CLOCK/CALENDAR
STICKER HERE
```

```
AFFIX FREE
MYSTERY GIFT
STICKER HERE
```

WE EVEN PROVIDE FREE POSTAGE!

It costs you *nothing* to send for your free books — we've paid the postage on the attached reply card. And we'll pick up the postage on your shipment of free books and gifts, and also on any subsequent shipments of books, should you choose to become a subscriber. Unlike many book clubs, we charge *nothing* for postage and handling!

Quickly Flynn told her what was wrong with the boy and why the surgery was necessary. By the time they reached the run-down house in a seedy neighborhood, she was well enough informed to help him try to convince the parents.

The Garcia family was expecting the *médico*. The inside of the house was spotless, and the father, mother and three children were dressed in their Sunday best. Mary Beth could see that they felt nervous and intimidated to be receiving a doctor in their home.

The conversation was conducted in Spanish, and when Flynn introduced her as Mrs. Warren, Mrs. Garcia smiled and said, "Oh, your wife."

Mary Beth waited for him to correct her, but when he didn't, she assumed he didn't feel it was necessary to explain that they were divorced.

Later when they left the Garcia home, Flynn had the consent form for the surgery signed by the parents.

As they got into the car, he sighed. "I owe you one, love. I'd never have been able to handle those people as easily as you did. You wouldn't like to come to work for me, would you?"

She grinned. "Sorry, Doctor, but I already have a job." The grin disappeared and she became serious. "They were just frightened, Flynn. They've only been in this country a couple of years and don't speak the language or understand the customs. They're terrified that their little son will die in that big impersonal hospital and it will somehow be their fault. All they needed was some tender, loving assurance."

He put his hand on her knee and caressed it. "Then it's no wonder you were so effective. You're an expert in tender, loving assurance."

He leaned over and kissed her briefly but firmly on the mouth, then removed his hand and started the engine. "It's too early for dinner," he said. "Why don't we take in a movie and eat later? I haven't been to the movies in months."

She was delighted that he wanted to spend the evening with her. "I'd love to. What show do you want to see?"

They stopped at the next market and bought a newspaper to find out what was playing. Huddled together in the car, they scanned the entertainment section and decided on a musical.

They held hands throughout the movie, and when it was over, Mary Beth had only a vague idea of what had happened on the screen; Flynn's nearness and the touch of his hand enclosing hers had been too distracting.

When they returned to the car, he asked her where she wanted to go for dinner.

"I couldn't possibly eat a big meal after all the junk food we've been munching on. Let's go to my apartment and fix hamburgers."

Flynn backed out of the parking space. "You don't have to cook them, we'll pick some up on the way."

Mary Beth laughed. "You can't fool me. You're afraid I'll burn them."

He grinned. "Not true, I just don't want to lose my reserved place in line at McDonald's. Now get with it, lady, and decide what you want from their extensive menu. I see the golden arches just ahead."

When they got back to the apartment, they sat on the sofa and divided the food between them. Mary Beth eyed Flynn's Big Mac and asked thoughtfully, "Have you eaten anything today?"

He nodded and swallowed the bite he was chewing. "I had breakfast about six o'clock this morning, but missed lunch."

"Why didn't you tell me you were hungry?" she asked, her guilt sounding in her voice. "We could have gone to a restaurant. I didn't mean to deprive you of a meal."

She'd been a doctor's wife long enough to know that they often missed meals during their busy days. Why hadn't she remembered and at least asked what he preferred, instead of thinking only of her own appetite?

"This is fine," he said reassuringly. "I'm glad you suggested it. I'd much rather be here. Do you realize this is the first time we've eaten alone together?"

She realized it only too well, but she knew she'd made a mistake in suggesting it. They were playing with fire, and if she got caught in the explosion, she'd have only herself to blame.

She got up and walked across the room to Peggy's stereo. "How about some background music? Do you like the National Symphony? I have their latest recording."

He looked at her appraisingly. "That would be great."

As the soft strains of Chopin floated on the air, she sat down and reached for her sandwich. Flynn had taken off his suit coat and loosened his tie. He looked comfortable sprawled against the back of the sofa, trying to sip his thick milk shake through a straw.

"Why did you buy this recording, Mary Beth?" he asked softly, and she knew she'd given herself away.

"It reminds me of the times we drove over to Washington to attend the National Symphony concerts." Her answer was simple and revealing.

He put his arm around her and held her against his side with her head resting on his shoulder. "I would not have thought you'd want to be reminded of the things we did together." His tone was rough with emotion.

"For a long time I didn't," she said. "That's one of the reasons I left the country. There were no memories in Spain, but shortly after I came back, I was passing a record shop and this album was displayed in the window. Some force stronger than my resistance propelled me into the store, and I brought it home and played it." She hesitated, then lowered her voice to a near whisper. "I cried all the way through it."

With a groan Flynn set his milk shake beside him and put his other arm around her. "You're braver than I am," he admitted. "I never again attended one of their concerts after you left. Grown men aren't allowed to cry in public places."

Just the thought of Flynn Warren, who had always seemed so self-sufficient, shedding tears because he missed her was almost her undoing. She put her sandwich down and raised her hand to cup his cheek. "Who said so? Men need the release of tears just as much as women do."

He turned his head and kissed her palm. "Maybe," he agreed, "but what I needed was you. I still do." He moved his hand under the purple sweater she wore with a matching skirt and caressed her breast through her lacy bra.

She felt the tremor that shook him as he struggled to control it, and an answering shiver buffeted her, further weakening what little resistance she had left.

No man but Flynn had been given the liberty to fondle her breasts, and she'd forgotten how good it felt. She leaned into his hand, and he lowered his mouth to nuzzle the spot under her jaw that only he knew was highly sensitive.

Vaguely she wondered if it was possible to die of pure bliss as he made little sucking movements against her skin, sending shivers through her. As he continued to stroke her breasts, she instinctively began unfastening the front of his shirt. It seemed to take forever to slip the small buttons out of the even smaller buttonholes, but finally the last one above his waistband popped open and she put both hands on his bare chest.

His sharp intake of breath was almost like a cry, and she jerked her hands away. "I'm sorry," she said. "I didn't mean to take liberties."

He took both her hands in one of his and put them back on his warm flesh. "Take all the liberties you like, sweetheart." His voice was raspy. "God, if you only knew how I've longed to feel your soft little hands on my body."

She relaxed against him again and rubbed her palms over his contracting muscles. He was still firm and slender, and when she touched his nipples she found that they were hard.

Unable to resist the next step in their well-remembered love play, she leaned down and circled one nipple with her tongue, then took it into her mouth and caressed it. Flynn's arms tightened around her, and his heart pounded against her face as he kneaded her throbbing breasts.

All the while she ignored the soft persistent voice of her conscience as it whispered, *Don't promise more than you intend to deliver.*

She knew she should put a stop to this—it was a no-win game they were playing. Still, was giving him the pleasure he asked for teasing just because it didn't end in ecstasy? Surely what they were doing wasn't wrong if it didn't go all the way. After all they'd once been married.

When she released the nipple to move across to the other one, he slid her sweater up and pulled it over her head, then tossed it aside, leaving her nude to the waist except for an abbreviated bra.

Her first instinct was to cover herself. It had been over three years since she'd been exposed to a man's gaze, and even with Flynn she felt shy. Before she could act, he released the catch on the bra and slid the straps from her arms, then finished removing his shirt.

"Come here," he said, and turned her so she was lying across his lap with her head on his shoulder. "Now, let's finish that kiss we started in your classroom this afternoon."

Briefly she fought against his mesmerizing tone even as she recognized the futility of her struggle. If he kissed her here in the privacy of her home the way he'd kissed her in the classroom this afternoon, she'd go up in smoke and there'd be no holding back, no second thoughts, no conscience to tell her no.

Flynn's hand rested on her nude flesh as he lowered his head and planted tiny kisses from her temple to her ear. "Please, Mary Beth." His voice was thick with desire. "Kiss me."

Her small store of resistance melted, and she raised her face to his. The fusion of their mouths was electrifying, and he ran his hand greedily over her bare breasts, teasing the nipples into peaks of desire. The small voice of her conscience was drowned out by the tempo of her thudding heart and the heat that swept through her in waves.

They drew their lips apart, then came together again and again in short, exhilarating nips. First she retreated and he conquered, then they reversed roles and she made him tremble with her tongue and her teeth and her teasing, half-formed kisses.

When the need to draw a deep breath became acute, they turned their heads away from each other, and she buried her face at the side of his throat while they both gasped for air.

"If that happens again, I won't be able to stop." His tone vibrated with frustration. "I'm not at all sure I can now."

The pressure of his hardness against her hip warned that he was telling the truth. She didn't want him to stop. She wanted to caress him intimately and make them both forget reason in their throbbing rush for fulfillment. She knew his need was urgent, and so was hers.

Before she could make a move one way or the other, the doorbell rang.

Mary Beth scrambled off Flynn's lap and he swore. She glanced at the clock on the wall. It was only eleven, but that had to be her roommate.

"It's Peg," Mary Beth hissed as she grabbed her sweater and pulled it over her head.

Flynn muttered something unprintable as he picked up his shirt and headed for the bathroom.

At some time during the evening she'd kicked off her shoes, but she didn't attempt to find them as she straightened her skirt and tucked loose strands of hair back into her French braid on her way to open the door.

Peggy was standing on the balcony, waiting patiently and looking contrite. "Sorry if I interrupted anything. I saw Flynn's car, but I didn't have anywhere else to go."

Mary Beth tried to look innocent and hoped her voice would work. "That's okay. I thought you were going to be late." She stood back so the other woman could come in.

"So did I," Peggy said, "but the guy I was with is an attorney, and he got a call on his beeper from one of his wealthy clients whose son had been arrested on a felony charge and needed a lawyer quick."

As she entered the room, both women spied an object that had obviously been tossed on the floor beside the sofa.

With a swooping movement Peggy gracefully picked up Mary Beth's bra and hid it behind one of the bright throw pillows. "Remember that for future reference," she said without judgment, and walked across the floor to disappear into her bedroom, leaving Mary Beth in an agony of embarrassment.

Flynn came out of the bathroom a few minutes later, once more neatly dressed in his shirt and tie. He walked over to the chair where he'd draped his suit coat and put it on.

He was leaving. Disappointment warred with relief in Mary Beth's battle-torn psyche. Her heart told her not to let the promise that had been interrupted slip away from her, but her head screamed that she was lucky to have escaped making a monumental mistake.

"Flynn, I'm sorry," she said miserably.

A tired smile touched the corners of his mouth. "So am I, sweetheart, but I suspect it's just as well. I don't want to seduce you. I want you to come to me willingly and fully aware of what you're doing."

He put his arm around her and walked her with him to the door. "I'm on call this weekend, but I'll be talking to you." He turned her toward him and put his other arm around her. "Now kiss me good-night."

She clasped him around the neck and raised her lips to his. Their mouths clung briefly before he lifted his head. "Enough," he said regretfully. "I'm not strong enough to stop a second time."

He kissed her again quickly, and then he was gone.

* * *

When Mary Beth and Peggy stepped out of the apartment early Monday morning to go to work, it was raining. The gentle, light rain seemed to bathe the world in a fresh green mist. It was a lovely way to start Thanksgiving week, and both women looked forward to the midsemester holiday.

Harry hadn't arrived yet when they got to the car, so Mary Beth started the engine and turned on the heater. The engine died. She started it again just as Harry came sprinting up and squeezed behind the passenger seat, where Peggy was sitting, to get into the back. Mary Beth shifted into reverse and started to back up, and the engine died again.

She swore, and Harry laughed. "Your foot's too dainty on the pedal, honey. Give it more gas. It's probably just cold and damp."

She did as he suggested, and the car shot out of the parking place, but when she shifted into first, it stalled again. Her language became more heated.

Harry sat forward in the seat. "Why don't you trade places with me and let me try it? I know a few words that might get it going."

Since it was a two-door sedan, they both got out before Mary Beth could climb into the back. Then Harry slid under the steering wheel. He stomped on the gas pedal a couple of times, then turned the key. The engine roared to life and purred contentedly as he shifted and drove toward the street.

"Do you want to trade places again?" he called over his shoulder.

"No, thanks," she answered disgustedly. "Go ahead and drive. We'll be lucky if we get to school on time as it is."

At the first busy intersection, the light was malfunctioning, and the blinking red light had traffic backed up for a quarter of a mile. All three of them were tense as the time ticked by.

Harry speeded up when they were finally on their way again, and just a block from the school a loud siren sounded behind them. Harry recited his extensive colorful vocabulary as the police car pulled them over to the curb.

The officer wasn't impressed with Harry's explanation of why he was speeding in a school zone, and demanded to see his driver's license, then wrote him a ticket before dismissing them.

"Sorry about that, ladies," Harry said as he jammed his wallet back into his uniform pants pocket. "I didn't realize I was over the speed limit."

After such a frustrating start, the rest of the day went smoothly, and by the time Mary Beth's classes were over and she'd straightened up her room, she'd put it out of her mind. It wasn't until she approached the usually dependable little Nissan that it occurred to her she might have trouble starting it again.

Peggy and Harry hadn't shown up yet so she slid into the driver's seat. Harry had pushed it way back to accommodate his long legs and she could hardly reach the pedals.

She bent over and reached down beneath the seat to feel for the lever so that she could adjust it. Darn, she never could remember where it was, but her fingers grazed a piece of paper on the floor just before they found it. She picked up the paper, which felt about two inches square, and held it in her hand as she pulled on the lever and scooted the seat forward to suit her.

When she sat up again, she saw Harry and Peggy coming toward her, and without looking at it, she stuffed the paper into her raincoat pocket to dispose of when she got home.

The car started immediately, and they arrived back at the apartment without mishap. Once there, Peggy didn't go inside, but got into her own car and drove off to keep a dental appointment. Mary Beth and Harry climbed the outside stairs together and let themselves into their connecting apartments.

She took off her coat and hung it up before she remembered the piece of paper she'd intended to dispose of. Reaching into the pocket, she withdrew a rumpled light green object that wasn't square, as it had felt, but rectangular and folded several times.

Curious, she unfolded it and discovered that it was a check made out to Harry Sullivan. It must have dropped out of his wallet that morning when he'd had to produce his driver's license for the police officer. Thank heaven, she hadn't tossed it out without looking at it. She'd better take it over to him before he missed it and began to worry.

As she started to refold it, she noticed the signature, and her fingers froze as she stared, dumbfounded.

It was signed by Dr. Flynn Warren!

Quickly her gaze flew to the top of the check, and there was Flynn's printed name and business address. Hesitantly, almost reluctantly, she looked at the amount, and her fists tightened, crumpling the paper even more.

It was dated three weeks ago and made out for five thousand dollars. At the bottom was written, *Advance for services*!

A surge of anger left her light-headed. She didn't even have to wonder what the money was for. Harry hadn't been hired by the school department to protect the children. He'd been hired by Flynn to keep an eye on her!

Damn him, he hadn't changed a bit! Even after three years on her own, he still thought she was too stupid to know how to take care of herself. He was manipulating her as surely as he always had, but now instead of doing so openly, he was being underhanded about it.

She banged her open palm against the closet doorjamb. Damn it all anyway. He'd had her almost convinced that he'd finally accepted her as a woman and cared about her as an adult rather than as a simpleminded child. Instead he'd actually hired a bodyguard for her!

Her rage was mixed with humiliation. Did anyone else know? Peggy? The school authorities?

Oh, dear Lord, how could he do this to her? His attitude could even have a harmful effect on her career. What school would hire a teacher whose ex-husband had a security guard following her everywhere she went?

Well, she'd put a stop to that in a hurry!

She picked up the phone, and her fingers shook with anger as she dialed the number printed on the check. "Dr. Warren's office, Judy speaking," said the youthful-sounding voice that answered.

"I must see Dr. Warren before he leaves the office," Mary Beth said. "Can you tell me how long he'll be there?"

The voice hesitated. "Doctor isn't scheduling any more appointments this afternoon. Is your child a regular patient?"

"This isn't a professional visit," Mary Beth said. "It's personal. Tell Flynn that Mary Beth called and not to leave the office until I get there."

She hung up and grabbed her coat and purse as she hurried out of the apartment, slamming the door behind her.

The late-afternoon traffic made for slow going on the freeway, and when she turned off it and headed toward the Scripps Memorial Hospital complex where Flynn had his offices, the city streets were even worse. The delays only increased her indignation, and she fumed and drummed her fingers on the steering wheel while she waited at every light.

It was getting dark by the time she spotted the hospital on the right. She turned into the grounds of the huge brick-and-stucco buildings, and deduced that the one to the west of the main structure was the medical offices.

A few minutes later, after reading Flynn's name and office number posted on the roster in the foyer, she took the elevator to the second floor. A rather lengthy search of the area finally brought her to the right door.

The waiting room was a child's delight, with a colorful clown mural on one wall and framed movie posters of Cinderella, E.T. and The Wizard of Oz on the others. The furniture, some nursery size and some adult, was sturdy, and there was an abundance of puzzles, games and children's books and magazines scattered around on the tables. In one corner a television was turned on to the Disney channel, but the room was empty.

Almost immediately a door opened and a pretty young woman wearing royal-blue slacks and a color-coordinated print blouse smiled. "May I help you?"

"I'm Mary Beth, the woman who called about an hour ago and left a message for Dr. Warren to wait for me. Is he still here?" Her tone was abrupt.

The woman nodded. "Yes. I gave him your message, and he said to show you into his private office as soon as you arrived. If you'll follow me please."

She led Mary Beth through a corridor and into a large, luxurious corner office. "Doctor's with a patient, but he won't be long. Please make yourself comfortable." She motioned toward the two thickly upholstered leather chairs in front of the large cherry wood desk. "Would you like a cup of coffee? Or maybe a glass of apple juice?"

This time Mary Beth managed a weak smile. "No, thank you. After battling the rush hour traffic, I'll just relax and try to unwind."

She did sit down, but as the minutes ticked by, she began to simmer. Her nerves were stretched too tight to relax, and she got up again and wandered around the room. One wall was lined with bookcases, which held Flynn's extensive medical library and a surprising number of legal reference books. There was also an up-to-date encyclopedia and a collection of periodicals.

On one shelf was a new picture of Flynn's father and mother that she'd never seen before. She picked it up and studied it through misty eyes. They were both smiling, but Edward looked thinner and a little gaunt. The malignancy he'd died of had apparently been taking its toll even then.

To think that she'd lived only a few miles from them for months before his death. If only she'd known, she could have had at least that little time with him again.

Her hand shook as she set the picture down. It was her own fault. If she hadn't been so stubborn about not getting in touch with Flynn...

An urgent voice behind her fractured her contemplation. "Mary Beth, what's the matter? Why did you want to see me here? Are you ill?"

She spun around to find Flynn, who wore a white lab coat, coming through the door, and her temporarily forgotten anger returned with a vengeance. "Ill?" Her voice was high and loud, and she lowered it. "How appropriate that you'd think I'd consult a pediatrician if I were ill. You'll never let me grow up, will you?"

Flynn blinked with surprise. "You needn't growl at me," he said mildly. "It was a perfectly logical question. You've never visited me at my office before, or anywhere else for that matter, so I naturally assumed that something was wrong."

Now he was being condescending, which infuriated her all the more. "Something is wrong," she snapped. "Perhaps you'd like to explain this." She reached into her coat pocket and handed him the folded check.

He unfolded it, then frowned. "Where did you get this?"

"It doesn't matter where I got it. What I want to know is what services is it an advance on?"

"Didn't Harry tell you?" he asked warily.

"Harry doesn't know I have it. I found it on the floor of the car, where he must have dropped it." She paused for a moment to catch her breath. "Did you hire him to spy on me?"

Flynn stared at her. "Of course not. I hired him to protect you."

"Protect me!" This time she actually screeched. "The only person I need protection from is you! You not only invade my personal space, but you've tampered with my civil rights."

He tried to interrupt, but she was too furious to notice. "Who appointed you my keeper? I let you off that hook three years ago when I divorced you. You have no right to have me followed without my knowledge or consent."

Flynn looked mutinous. "You're my wife, dammit. It's not only my right but my obligation to protect you when you insist on putting yourself in danger—"

"Why do you keep ignoring the fact that I divorced you three years ago? I'm not your wife! I'm not your ward. I'm not anything to you, and I promise you, Flynn, if Harry Sullivan doesn't move out of my apartment complex tonight and stay as far away from me as he can get, I'll get an injunction to force you to leave me alone."

She rushed out of the office, leaving him staring after her in open-mouthed amazement.

Chapter Seven

By the time Mary Beth got back to the apartment, much of her rage had dissipated. She'd vented most of it on Flynn, and the rest had seeped away as she once more battled rush hour traffic on her way home. Peggy had dinner ready, and as they ate, Mary Beth told her what had happened and where she'd been.

"I never did trust that situation," Peg said. "There were too many coincidences."

"I know you didn't," Mary Beth answered. "I should have listened to you instead of being so sure my judgment was infallible. Good grief, you'd think I'd learn after all the errors I've made."

"Don't start whipping yourself," the other woman admonished. "Harry's a trained professional in making people think he's something he's not. Don't be too hard on Flynn, either. At least he cared enough to make sure you were safe. I've never known a man who'd go that far for me."

Mary Beth sighed. "You don't want to, either, unless he's your father or your guardian. Believe me, it's demeaning to have the man you love treat you like an incompetent nincompoop. Bodyguard indeed." She stirred her coffee. "I just hope the word never gets around the school, if it hasn't already."

Peggy smiled. "Oh, I don't know. I think it's pretty romantic. How many women do you know who have their own Prince Charming riding to the rescue?"

Mary Beth grunted. "Flynn's no Prince Charming, and I'm sure not Cinderella. This is the last straw, Peg. I'm not going to see him anymore. He'll always think of me as the waif he rescued from the jungle. That was enough for me once, but not now. Much as I love him—"

The peal of the doorbell interrupted her, and Peggy got up to answer it. "If it's Flynn I won't see him," Mary Beth called after her. But it wasn't Flynn, it was Harry Sullivan.

He followed Peggy back into the kitchen and stood with his uniform hat in his hand, looking sheepish. "I—I guess you know I've been fired," he said without looking at either of them.

Mary Beth felt a mixture of annoyance and embarrassment and looked down at her plate as Peggy resumed her seat across the table. "Go away, Harry, I don't want to talk to you."

"Aw, come on, honey—"

"I'm not your honey," she snapped.

"All right then, *Mrs.* Warren," he said with exasperation.

She raised her head and looked at him. "It's *Ms.* Warren, and I don't enjoy being made a fool of. I thought you were my friend."

Harry frowned. "I am your friend, that's why I'm here. Dr. Warren's hot as hell about me being careless with that check. Can't say that I blame him. Stuffing it in my billfold and forgetting to deposit it was a stupid thing to do. I wish you'd brought it to me, though, and given me a chance to cool you down a bit before you blasted him about it. He's a nice guy, Mary Beth, and you've no cause to be so hard on him. He only wanted to make sure you weren't mugged or raped."

She cringed. "Not that it's any of your business, Harry, but I've managed to survive for twenty-four years with no harm done. I exercise reasonable caution, and I've had classes in self-defense. I don't need a strongman following me everyplace I go. Tell me, did you enjoy my date with Don MacGregor last week? I suppose you told Flynn everything we did."

A sly teasing smile lit his face. "Sorry I missed it. My instructions were not to intrude on your social life, but now I'm wondering what you and this Don did that you didn't want the doc to know about."

Rage once more swept through Mary Beth, and she jumped to her feet. "Why you . . . you voyeur!"

Harry reached her in one long step and caught her by the shoulders. "Hey, lighten up. I was only kidding."

It was Peggy's voice that ripped through the racket and silenced them. "Cut it out, both of you! Harry, you deserved that. She's upset, you had no business teasing her. Mary Beth, pull yourself together and stop treating this thing like a tragedy. Now let's all sit down and try to talk calmly."

Harry jammed his hat on his head. "Sorry, Doc says I'm to get my tail out of here tonight, so I'm taking off. I just wanted to say goodbye and try to make peace with little Miss Independence here." He indicated a smoldering Mary Beth. "That doesn't seem very likely so I'll be on my way, but I want to leave you with a word of warning. If anything happens to either one of you pretty ladies, Doc and I are gonna take it personally, and we won't sit around waiting for the police to catch the sleazeball and slap his wrist. I guarantee you that the way we handle it will be a hell of a lot more embarrassing to you than just having a grizzled old security guard tagging after you."

Without waiting for a reply, he turned and stomped out.

Mary Beth slept little that night. She was still angry, but now the anger was mixed with guilt, and that made her all the madder. She'd had every right to express her feelings to both Flynn and Harry. They'd treated her like a three-year-old who couldn't be trusted not to play in the street.

She couldn't get comfortable in the bed, and turned from her right to her left side.

Flynn had totally disregarded her right to privacy. He hadn't even consulted her about his desire to protect her, but in his usual high-handed manner had been sure he knew what was best. The man was insufferable!

Still, she regretted the way she'd treated Harry. After all, he was only doing his job, and she'd gotten him fired.

Restlessly she rolled back to her right side again.

Well, not exactly fired. The case, or whatever it was called, had been terminated at her insistence, but it was no reflection on the security guard.

She should have been kinder when he came by to apologize and say goodbye. He didn't have to do that. He could have just left without a word and saved himself a tongue-lashing. Mary Beth had liked Harry. He'd been a nice guy, and she'd enjoyed having him for a car-pool rider and next-door neighbor.

Rising up, she plumped the pillow into a more comfortable shape.

Darn it all, why did she always have to see both sides of an argument? Why couldn't she just hate Flynn and Harry and feel vindicated by her sharp-tongued harangue instead of regretting her impulsive fireworks?

She had a right to be furious. Any woman would be, under the circumstances, so why did she feel so guilty?

The following day, Tuesday, had been a grueling one for Flynn, with a morning spent in emergency surgery patching up a ten-year-old boy whose bicycle was hit by a speeding car, and an afternoon in his office trying to catch up on appointments. It was after seven before the last little patient left and he could collapse in the big comfortable executive chair behind his desk and close his eyes.

He'd spent most of the previous night pacing the floor and cursing first Harry for his carelessness, then Mary Beth for being so bullheaded, and finally himself for setting the whole mess in motion. It had seemed like a good idea at the time. He'd been terrified for her safety in an area where crack houses and prisonlike lockups on schools were a way of life.

He'd known she wouldn't approve of his hiring a bodyguard for her. That's why he hadn't told her, but he hadn't expected her to be so outraged when she found out. Dammit, she should be grateful that he was willing to protect her.

His musing was interrupted by his nurse, who stuck her head into the office to tell him she was leaving to go home. "You'd better do the same," she said in her warm, friendly way.

"I'll do that," he said.

He didn't leave immediately, however. First he picked up the phone and dialed Mary Beth's number.

Luck was with him, and the voice on the other end was Peggy's. "Peg, this is Flynn. I want to talk to you, but I don't want Mary Beth to know. Are you alone?"

"Yes," she said in her husky voice. "She's cleaning up the kitchen and I'm on the cordless phone. I'm taking it to my room."

A few seconds later he heard a door close, then Peggy's voice again. "Okay, Flynn, I can talk without being overheard, but if you want me to intervene for you with Mary Beth, it won't work. I've already tried and got shot down for my trouble."

He sighed. "Thanks for your efforts, but that's not what I was going to ask of you. I need to talk to her, but she'll never agree to see me, so I'm coming over unannounced. I just don't want to drive all that way to find she's not at home. Do you know if she has any plans to go out this evening?"

Peggy seemed to hesitate. "Is this an underhanded way of finding out if she's dating another man?" Her tone was cool.

Flynn's wasn't, and he barked an oath into the telephone. "Sorry," he apologized, "but such a thing never crossed my mind. I guess I deserve your suspicion, though."

"Yes, you do, but I believe you," she said. "Mary Beth will be home all evening, but I can't guarantee that she'll be civil to you."

He ran his hand through his hair. "I'm sure she won't. The best I can hope for is that she'll listen and try to understand my side. I should be there in about an hour."

* * *

Mary Beth shut the dishwasher door and turned on the switch, then straightened and rubbed the tight, aching muscles of her lower back. Now that she'd finally cooled down and was no longer running on the adrenaline of pure rage, she was exhausted. She felt battered both physically and emotionally.

She hadn't slept the night before. Her fury had acted like a drug-induced high that kept her mind and her body in perpetual motion, feeding on her outrage and rendering her unable to relax.

It wasn't until this morning when she and Peggy had driven to school without Harry that her artificial energy began to sag. During the day, several teachers and some of the children remarked about his absence and assumed he was sick. Mary Beth hadn't commented, but as the day had progressed she'd become more and more depressed until now she was as "down" as she had been "up" last night.

Dragging herself into the living room, she slumped onto the couch. The comfortable old jeans and shirt she'd changed into when she got home made her even more relaxed, and she tucked her feet under her, pulled one of the throw pillows behind her head and closed her eyes. Maybe she would rest for a few minutes before going over her lesson plans for the next day.

She was wakened by someone rubbing her shoulder and speaking in a soft masculine voice against her ear. "Wake up, sleepyhead." A familiar light kiss caressed her cheek, and she smiled and leaned into it.

"Come on, sweetheart," the voice whispered as the mouth trailed kisses down her face. "Wake up and talk to me."

She was floating through thick, dark layers of sleep, reaching for the voice but unable to find the light.

Gentle fingers stroked her wispy bangs back to make room on her forehead for the teasing mouth, and involuntarily she lifted her head to meet it. She missed the mark, and her lips landed on a chin that was rough with a late-day stubble.

The contact speeded her ascent to wakefulness, and she opened her eyes to find Flynn's face barely an inch from hers. His brown eyes were dark with emotion as he shifted just enough to brush her mouth with his, sending a tremor through her and bringing tears of bitterness.

Quickly she sat up, and it was then that she realized he was hunkered down beside her. He stood, then sat on the couch next to her, but she jumped up and walked away as she strove to gather her wits about her.

"Oh, come on now, Flynn?" she asked angrily. "You say you don't want to seduce me, but you don't mind taking advantage of me while I'm asleep."

A sob escaped her, but she pressed her hands into her eyes to keep the tears from falling.

She heard him get up and stand behind her, but he didn't touch. "You'll have to forgive me," he said, "but I couldn't help it. In sleep you look just like the wife I used to have who welcomed my caresses."

Her fists clenched as his words slashed through her. "You mean the one you destroyed with your lies and deceit?"

She heard him draw in his breath and knew she'd retaliated successfully, but the fact brought her no triumph. The fight had been drained out of her, leaving only despair.

"Yes, I suppose I did," he answered wearily, "but I didn't come here to quarrel. Can't we sit down and talk?"

Mary Beth was finally fully awake, and she looked around. "How did you get in? And where's Peggy?"

"Peg let me in and then went to her room. She said to tell you that if you needed her just to holler."

Mary Beth nodded. "Believe me, I will." She beckoned toward the sofa. "Sit down. I suppose we do have loose ends to tie up. The coffee's hot, would you like a cup?"

"Yes, please," he said. "Do you have some cookies or crackers to go with it? I haven't eaten since breakfast."

She tried to ward off the flash of concern that always tormented her when she knew he wasn't taking care of himself, but it was a losing battle. "You're a doctor, for heaven's sake," she snapped. "You know what can happen if you don't eat properly. Why do you skip meals? You'd done the same thing last time you were here." She turned and walked toward the kitchen.

"I don't usually," he said as he walked along with her, "but I had an emergency surgery this morning that threw the whole day off. I didn't realize I'd missed lunch until it was past time for dinner."

In the kitchen she motioned him toward the table and poured him a cup of coffee, then put the lasagna left over from dinner into the microwave oven and tossed a small salad. He protested that she shouldn't go to so much trouble, but when she put the food before him, he ate every bite and even polished off a big dish of ice cream.

As she sipped her coffee and watched him eat, Mary Beth was acutely aware that if he hadn't wanted to talk to her, he'd have gone right home from the office and enjoyed a hot nourishing meal before settling down for a restful evening. Instead he'd battled traffic to come to her, settled for a makeshift meal, and they would probably quarrel again before he started the long drive home just in time to fall into bed, provided he wasn't called out on another emergency.

He looked tired. She would have seen that right away if she hadn't been so wrapped up in her own feelings. He probably hadn't slept much better than she had last night, but it hadn't stopped him from putting in a long day at his practice and then trying to straighten things out with her tonight.

When he'd finished eating, they returned to the living room, where Flynn sat down on the sofa and Mary Beth took a chair several feet away from him.

After a few moments of uncomfortable silence, he finally spoke. "I'm sorry you're so angry because I hired Harry to look after you."

She winced. "That's not what you're supposed to be sorry about," she said. "You should be sorry that you don't have enough faith in me to trust me to look after myself. You should be even sorrier that you hired a bodyguard without consulting me. You had no right to invade my privacy that way."

Flynn shook his head sadly. "That was never my intention. I specifically told Harry not to spy, just to make sure you were safe going to and from school and while you were on the job. I hate the thought of you wandering around in that area alone. Have you any idea what the crime rate is down there?"

"Of course I have," she said impatiently. "How could I not? I'm there every day, but none of the teachers have ever been molested. We don't 'wander around alone,' as you put it. We seldom leave the school from the time we get there until we leave to go home, and we have one full-time security guard. I'm appalled at being singled out for protection. You'd have put the money to better use by hiring a second guard for the whole school."

"But that's exactly what I did," he pointed out. "During school hours, Harry functioned in the same capacity as the other guard. The school was getting two security guards for the price of one."

She was startled into silence. She'd never thought of it that way, but it made sense.

"I suppose you're right," she said, reluctant to admit there was anything acceptable about the arrangement, "but that doesn't make it honorable."

"When did a man's desire to protect his loved ones become dishonorable?" he asked quietly.

For the first time, Mary Beth didn't have a snappy answer. "I . . . I'm not your loved one, and you're twisting my words."

"No, I'm not. I want to know why I'm the villain because I care too much to stand by and not try to protect you when you deliberately place yourself in danger."

"I don't—"

"Yes, you do. I admire your courage and dedication, but you'll have to admit that you teach in one of the most unsafe districts in San Diego. You could work in any other school and be safer."

"I suppose so," she admitted, "but I'm needed at El Dorado. That's the district with the largest concentration of Spanish-speaking families, and it's difficult to get qualified instructors to come there."

"That's because the school looks like a prison and is just about as safe. In the past year both rapes and muggings were up twenty-five percent, and trafficking in drugs is a common occurrence."

She eyed him suspiciously. "How do you know that? And come to think of it, how were you able to get Harry on school property to guard me?"

Flynn shrugged. "A little influence can pull a lot of strings. I have contacts on the school board, but even though I was paying Harry's salary, I had to agree that he would be employed as a school guard during school hours. Dammit, Mary Beth, let me rehire him as a second guard at El Dorado.''

She shook her head vigorously, but before she could say no, he stopped her. "Now wait and hear me out. He doesn't have to live next door if you don't want him to. He can stop by for you and Peg in the mornings and drop you off in the afternoons, but during the day, he will be working for the school even though I pay his salary.''

The idea was repellent. "Absolutely not. We both know that if you pay his salary, he'd be working for you, and his priority would be me. You can imagine what the other teachers would say if they knew I was getting special attention.''

"You wouldn't be getting special attention,'' he said patiently. "All the teachers would be safer with Harry there. Surely they were relieved when he started work two weeks ago.''

She couldn't deny his reasoning, and it was true that the teachers had been pleased when a second security man was added to the staff. The neighborhood had been deteriorating for years, and everyone agreed that it was only a matter of time until the situation between the street gangs and the school officials erupted into violence. Was she wrong to be so obstinate?

"I hadn't considered it that way,'' she admitted. "But even if I thought it were necessary, I'd never let you spend that much money on my welfare. Why can't you understand that I'm not your responsibility anymore, Flynn?''

"Probably for the same reason you can't understand that you'll always be my responsibility. I doubt that we'll ever agree on that, but please don't let it come between us. Surely we can work around it.''

"We probably could if you'd cooperate, but not as long as you pull underhanded stunts like this last one. I trust you with my life, but I no longer trust you with my emotions. You've abused that trust too flagrantly, and we can't build any kind of relationship without it. Right now all I want is for you to leave me alone. You're suffocating me."

She saw in his unguarded expression the naked pain her harsh words had caused him, and it reflected back to torment her.

When he spoke, his pain sounded in his voice. "I'm sorry, sweetheart, but I can't do that. I swear to you, though, that I'll never again interfere in your life, or make decisions that concern you, without discussing them with you."

Mary Beth could have wept. Such a beautiful promise, but it was meaningless. "That would have meant a lot to me at one time, Flynn." The anguish in her tone echoed the pain in his. "Unfortunately, now I just don't believe you."

He groaned and covered his face with his hands, and the gesture made her ache to comfort him. What a masochistic fool she was! If she wasn't careful, she'd wake up some morning and find that she'd lost all her hard-won independence and was once more Flynn Warren's submissive little girl who never made a move without his approval.

She could never be happy living like that again, but, dear God, she'd learned from experience that living without him was a form of hell.

The sound of his voice mercifully interrupted her thoughts. "Then I'll just have to prove to you that I mean it. Have you made plans for Thanksgiving?"

She blinked, thrown off balance by the abrupt change of subject. Flynn was once more composed, and his expression was bland. "Thanksgiving? No, not exactly. Peggy and Don have invited me to have dinner with them at their parents' home, but it's a family gathering and I don't like to intrude."

"Then spend it with me," he said eagerly. "I'll be alone, too. Lars insists on cooking dinner for me even though he won't be eating it. He has other plans."

His invitation took her completely by surprise. "Oh, I . . . I don't think so, Flynn. . . ."

"Don't turn me down, Mary Beth. I know you're angry with me, but neither of us has family here. . . ."

His voice broke, and she was out of her chair before she realized what she was doing. How could she have forgotten that this Thanksgiving would be especially difficult for him? She doubted that he'd ever spent a holiday alone before, and with his father so recently dead . . .

She managed to get hold of herself and sit down beside him, but without touching. "All right," she said, and silently cursed herself for giving in so easily after deciding not to date him anymore. "I'll spend the day with you, and thanks for asking me, but understand that I'm not promising anything but my company for a few hours. I'm afraid that a relationship between us is unwise and self-defeating. We just hurt each other."

He reached out and carefully took her hand. "The last thing I ever want to do is hurt you, Mary Beth, but in my bumbling way I manage to do it anyhow. I won't make any demands on you Thursday. We'll just talk and eat and listen to records. Maybe take a walk on the beach. Would you like that?"

She was acutely aware of his hand holding hers, his delight that she'd spend time with him and his eagerness to please her. She didn't doubt but that his emotions were genuine, but so were they when he was cold and overbearing.

He was such an enigma. Like two different personalities in the same body. Sometimes the adoring lover, other times the disapproving guardian. She was never sure which man she was dealing with.

He squeezed her hand, and she knew he was waiting for an answer to his question. "I'd like it very much," she said.

Flynn looked at his watch and frowned. "It's late and you have to get up early in the morning. I'd better be going."

He stood, still holding her hand, and pulled her up with him. "Thank you for not throwing me out when you woke up and found me here," he said huskily as they walked to the door.

She turned the lock and opened it. For a minute they stood there just inches apart, looking at each other. The expression on his face was one of tenderness and desire.

He's going to kiss me, she thought as conflicting emotions churned inside her. Her good sense told her to pull away, while her love for him ached for the touch of his mouth covering hers.

It was Flynn who proved the stronger of the two as, with obvious reluctance, he turned and walked briskly away.

Chapter Eight

Mary Beth woke Thursday morning with mixed feelings—excitement at the prospect of being with Flynn again and seeing his home, and a nagging suspicion that she was making a mistake that would cost her dearly.

Peggy, good friend that she was, remained neutral on the subject and refused to give advice. She left for her parents' home early in order to spend more time with relatives who had come from out of town, and Mary Beth had the apartment to herself.

Flynn had offered to pick her up, but she'd insisted on driving. She wanted her car available in case things between them got out of hand and she had to make a hurried exit.

Dinner was being served at three o'clock so Lars would have time to spend part of the day with friends, but Flynn had asked her to come as early as she could. He'd said to dress casually, so she chose a loose-fitting royal-blue cotton dress with a wide flounce at the bottom. She'd bought it in Spain, and it was heavily hand-embroidered. A fun dress for an informal day at home. With it, she wore matching flats.

She brushed her blond hair until it gleamed, and was strongly tempted to leave it to fall around her shoulders for Flynn. Regretfully she abandoned the idea and fashioned the French braid instead. Being alone with him in his home was dangerous enough; she wasn't going to tantalize him and then act the outraged innocent when he followed through.

It was nearly one o'clock when she arrived at Flynn's address and pulled into the driveway. The garage and a red-tiled roof behind it were the only parts of the house visible from the street; the rest of it backed up to the cliff and fronted on the ocean. Beachfront property in La Jolla, for heaven's sake. It must be worth a fortune!

He'd apparently been watching for her, because he appeared from around the side of the garage as she opened the car door and stepped out. *"Mia bella querida,"* he said softly with an admiring smile as he approached her. "I know I've never seen that dress before. I like it."

"Thank you," she answered tremulously as her gaze clung to his. She knew she should be more reserved, but he'd called her his beautiful darling. How could she not respond emotionally?

Today he was wearing dark brown slacks with a matching brown shirt and a lightweight beige sweater. He looked absolutely smashing. "You didn't tell me you lived right on the beach," she added to cover her embarrassment when she realized she was staring.

"Didn't I? I guess the subject never came up." He reached out and took her arm. "There are stairs around here at the side of the house that lead down to the front."

They descended the flagstone steps, which were cut into the side of the cliff and nearly hidden by green leafy ground cover and colorful hibiscus and bougainvillea. The building was brick-and-wood Spanish-style architecture with a front courtyard enclosed by a wrought iron fence that didn't interfere with the sweeping view of the beach and ocean, yet provided desired privacy.

Mary Beth stopped so she could gaze at it. "It's a beautiful home, Flynn. Oh, and the second-floor rooms even have French doors leading onto the balcony."

"Yes," he said, "and we have the Pacific ocean for a swimming pool. I'm sorry I didn't tell you to bring a bathing suit."

She shivered. "It's okay. Weather in the high sixties isn't warm enough to entice me into the ocean. Especially if the Pacific is as cold as the Atlantic."

He laughed. "I'm afraid it is. Come on, then, I'll show you the inside of the house and introduce you to Lars." He held the gate open to let her pass. "Maybe I'd better prepare you for my housekeeper. He looks like a hulking brute, but the only way he'd hurt you is if you wrestle with him."

She grinned. "In that case I'll try to restrain myself."

The double front doors were a heavy dark walnut with stained glass windows. Mary Beth gasped softly and reached out to touch the glowing glass with her fingers. "Oh, Flynn, how magnificent. They should be in a museum."

She looked up at him and saw the tenderness in his eyes. "They're not quite museum quality, but I did commission them from one of the leading artists in Italy. I remembered how much you admired the church windows in Baltimore and Washington. We attended so many different churches that I almost forgot which one we belonged to, but you weren't listening to the sermons, you were admiring the windows.''

A warm glow pervaded her. He'd been thinking of her when he decorated his home! Was it possible that he really hadn't wanted the divorce? Had she made a tragic mistake by leaving the country instead of staying in Baltimore and trying to work things out with him?

These were questions that needed to be answered, and she resolved to ask them before she left here today.

When he unlocked the doors and ushered her inside, it was like stepping back in time to the years she'd spent in Spain. The big open rooms, high oblong windows and archways were all accentuated in rich dark woods. The entryway, living room and dining room flowed gracefully into one another.

The floor in the entryway was tiled, and the gleaming hardwood of the other rooms was left uncarpeted, with colorful handwoven rugs placed in strategic areas.

She uttered a little gasp of delight. ''Oh, Flynn, it's exactly right. So...so homey. And the fireplace...'' She walked over to the stone fireplace that nearly covered one wall.

A crackling fire blazed merrily, and the aroma of roasting turkey wafted on the air. A basket of beautifully arranged asters and chrysanthemums in autumn shades of gold, brown and orange interspersed with green leaves sat on the high, thick plank that served as a mantel.

''I love it,'' she said in a throaty whisper.

''I was sure you would,'' he answered from directly behind her, then carefully clasped her shoulders and eased her back against him. ''That's why I bought it.''

A painful knot of tears for what might have been formed in her throat, and her eyes burned as she blinked to keep them from falling. "Please don't make me cry," she pleaded.

His hands moved down her arms and crossed at her waist. "I won't," he whispered in her ear as he gently rocked them both. "I want today to be a happy one for us."

It was then that she realized how hungry she'd been for his embrace. Even when she was furious with him, she subconsciously longed for his touch. Leaning her head back against his shoulder, she covered his hands with her own. "So do I," she murmured as she adjusted her breathing to the rise and fall of his chest.

For a moment the security of Flynn's arms around her, the feel of his familiar body pressed against her back and the touch of his cheek as it gently rubbed her own created a sense of enchantment. It surrounded them and brought a warm glow of relief, relaxing the tenseness that had gripped Mary Beth ever since their quarrel.

Flynn, too, was caught in the spell. Mary Beth's sweet response to him was pure heaven. She was all woman, soft and fragrant and warm, but he was discovering a core of steel within her that hadn't been there before.

She no longer needed him the way she had in the beginning, and that saddened him. He seemed to have a paternal compulsion to be needed. That's probably what had motivated him to choose pediatrics over other medical specialties, but he also had a budding respect for her new independence.

She thought he'd betrayed her. Maybe he had, but not in the way she assumed. If only he could find a way to make her trust him again. He tried so hard, but every move he'd made toward her had turned into a disaster.

He couldn't let her go, but neither would he attempt to keep her against her will. She would probably eventually forgive him for the bodyguard debacle, but there was an even more forbidding hurdle to be endured.

A shudder rippled through him, and his arms involuntarily tightened around her. If only he'd been truthful with her immediately after his father's memorial service. True, she would have been furious, but each day he'd waited since then dwindled the chance that she'd ever forgive him. Now, after more than three weeks...

With a herculean effort he restrained himself from broaching the troubling topic. Not today! These could be the last peaceful hours he'd spend with her. Tomorrow he'd confess his duplicity, but today was going to be perfect.

He lowered his head and kissed the side of her throat. "Do you remember the first Thanksgiving after we were married?" His voice was unsteady.

Remember? Mary Beth's heart pounded with the memory. That was the night they'd finally consummated their marriage.

"I'm not likely to ever forget," she murmured shakily. "The emotions you were building in me were so...so new and strong that I thought surely I must be going to die. Then, when...when it happened...I knew that I had died and was being catapulted straight to heaven."

With a groan he turned her in his arms and pressed her against him. "I'd never experienced anything quite like it, either," he murmured into her hair. "I didn't realize until then that having sex and making love were two different things."

She raised her head to look at him. "Were you making love with me, Flynn?"

He moved one of his hands over her back, lighting fires as he did. "Always," he said raggedly. "Don't you know that, sweetheart? Every time with you was special and new and incredibly erotic."

The question of whether it had been special and erotic with Vanessa, too, tormented her, but she couldn't ask about that. If it had been, she didn't want to know. If it hadn't, the very asking would have broken the spell anyway.

A beeping sound finally penetrated their absorption, and Mary Beth recognized it as Flynn's pager. "Damn," he muttered as he released her and reached into his pocket. "I'm not on call. Excuse me a minute, honey."

He walked across the room and picked up the telephone while she wandered over to the front window and gazed dreamily out at the narrow strip of beach and the green water beyond. Restless waves broke into white foam in their frenzied dash to throw themselves on the sand, then withdrew to be replaced by an endless supply of others.

In the quiet of the room, she could hear the muted roar and the splash of the dancing water through the open windows. There was a natural rhythm to the waves that was almost hypnotic if one watched and listened long enough, and she jumped when Flynn touched her on the shoulder from behind.

"Sorry, I didn't mean to startle you," he said. "That was the hospital. They haven't been able to contact the doctor who's supposed to be on call for me today, but I think we've got everything under control."

He took her hand in his. "Come on. I'll show you the kitchen. Maybe Lars can round up something for us to nibble on. The smell of turkey is making me hungry."

They crossed the dining room and pushed open the swinging door to the kitchen. It was huge with a butcher block island in the center and gleaming copper and steel pots and pans hanging above it. The cabinets were of the same dark wood as in the rest of the house, but the curtains and all the major appliances were a bright sunshine yellow that seemed to bring the outdoors inside.

Standing at the sink under the window that overlooked the north side of the house was a square hulk of a man, who turned to them with what Mary Beth could only describe as a snarl. But it wasn't a snarl. Almost immediately she recognized it as his version of a smile. His battered features, probably from too many years spent in the ring, made him the only truly ugly man she'd ever seen.

"Come on in," he said in a low, raspy voice as he turned off the running water. "I was just about to bring in the munchies and drinks." He motioned to a large silver tray loaded with raw vegetable slices, chips and dips.

Flynn introduced him, and Lars wiped his huge hands on the white wraparound apron that covered his stocky frame before holding one out to Mary Beth. "Been lookin' forward to meetin' you," he said, but she noticed that the smile didn't go all the way to his colorless gray eyes when he looked at her.

She could feel the leashed power in him as he briefly held her hand, and she knew that, had he wanted to, he could easily have crushed it with little more than a flexing of his muscles.

He was rather frightening. Although no taller than Flynn's six feet, his wide shoulders, barrel chest and hard, rippling biceps made him seem immense. His bullet-shaped head was also larger than usual and totally bald.

He picked up the tray and led the way into the living room, where he set it down on the coffee table between the sofa and the fireplace, then went back into the kitchen. Flynn and Mary Beth sat down on the couch, and Lars returned almost immediately with two squat crystal glasses of tomato juice with a celery stick protruding from each.

"Here you are," he said as he handed them the drinks. "Although why you'd want spiced tomato juice without any vodka is beyond me. Dinner'll be ready in about an hour." He turned and walked away.

Mary Beth laughed and sipped her drink. "I guess we teetotalers will always be oddities," she observed.

Flynn reached for a handful of potato chips. "I suppose so, but I saw the grisly results of drinking and driving when I did my stint in the hospital emergency room during training. I also see a lot of families broken up because of alcohol in my practice. It's just not worth the price—"

The loud beep of his pager interrupted him, and with a grimace he reached into his pocket to turn it off. "Sorry again," he said as he stood, "but I have to answer it."

She nodded, and he crossed the room and picked up the phone. After a few terse words he put it down again and returned to stand beside the couch. He looked angry and frustrated. "I'm sorry, sweetheart, but they still haven't found that idiot who's supposed to be covering for me. He'd better have a good excuse, but meanwhile I'm going to have to run over to the hospital and take care of this myself."

She swallowed her disappointment. "Of course you do," she said gently as she stood up.

He put his arms around her and drew her close. "I hate having to leave you. Feel free to wander around. I have several televisions, VCRs, a stereo system..."

She looked up at him and smiled. "I'll be fine. I'm used to this. I used to be a doctor's wife, remember."

"There's no way I could ever forget," he murmured as he lowered his head and captured her mouth.

Flynn left, and Mary Beth wandered through the beautifully decorated but lonely rooms. Almost everything was new since she'd lived with him, but occasionally she spotted an article that had been in their home in Baltimore: the fine old Spanish altar cross they'd salvaged from the mission in Central America; the Christmas cactus she'd bought him on their first Christmas was still planted in the pot she'd thrown in her college ceramics class; the monstrously expensive painting of the ragged little girl standing amid the rubble of an unknown disaster with all the anguish of the ages staring out of her huge, expressive eyes. They'd found it in a tiny gallery on a side street in London where they'd gone to spend their second wedding anniversary and had both fallen in love with it.

All brought memories she'd carefully locked away flooding back, and the pain hadn't dimmed with the years. She wondered what had happened to all their other things.

It was while she was pondering this agonizing question that a thundering crash and a loud yell from the kitchen sent her scurrying toward the noise. She pushed open the swinging door with both hands, then stopped, letting it swing shut as she surveyed the scene before her.

The floor was covered with water from which steam was still rising, and a heavy copper cooking pot, which was obviously the cause of the crash, was turned upside down by the center island. But it was Lars, sitting off to one side on the wet tile, holding his right leg and muttering curses that galvanized her into action.

"Lars, my God, what happened? Are you hurt?" She rushed across the room and knelt down on the hot wet floor beside him.

"I slipped and dropped a pan of boiling water," he said between clenched teeth. "Now get out of here. This is none of your concern."

She could see that his pants leg was drenched. Some of the scalding water had obviously spilled on him.

She looked around and spotted a set of wicked-looking knives sheathed in a wooden block on the counter. Jumping up, she hurried gingerly across the slippery floor to snatch one of them and returned to again kneel beside him.

He took one look at the knife she held above his leg and roared. "What are you going to do with that?"

She clutched the bottom of his pants. "Hold still. I'm going to cut this hot material away before it burns you more."

Thank heaven the jeans weren't skintight, and she was able to hold them away from his ankle as she jabbed the knife into the tough denim and sliced awkwardly downward through the thick hem.

In a lightning-quick movement Lars clutched her wrist and twisted it, sending the knife flying in one direction and Mary Beth in another. "Like hell you are," he snarled. "You'll do more damage than the scalding water did." Grabbing the two ends of the cut material, he effortlessly ripped it to midthigh, exposing a muscled leg that was turning bright red.

She'd been thrown off balance from her kneeling position and landed heavily on her bottom, then on her back. For a moment she was too surprised to speak, and as she rolled over onto her stomach to get up, she realized that she was wallowing in water that was still uncomfortably hot.

Deciding that she was wasting time trying to help the obstinate giant, she got to her feet and walked to the telephone.

"Who are you calling?" he demanded from behind her, and she was aware that he still hadn't tried to get up off the floor.

"Nine-one-one," she said as she lifted the phone. "They'll send an ambulance."

"Dammit, woman, will you get out of my kitchen and leave me alone! It's just a burn. I can take care of it myself. I'm not goin' to no hospital, and the paramedics can't treat me here without my permission. Now put down that phone."

His tirade was peppered with obscenities that Mary Beth chose not to acknowledge, but she couldn't ignore the truth of his statement. There was no use summoning an emergency crew if he wouldn't allow himself to be treated.

She hung up the phone and turned to look at him. "I'm sorry if I annoy you, Lars, but you've been badly burned. If Flynn were here, he'd know what to do, but he may not be back for quite a while, and I have no way of gauging how serious it is. Please let me get you some help."

He was still holding his leg and gritting his teeth. "If you want to feel useful, get me a pan of ice water and a towel."

She went to the sink and ran cold water into a large kettle, then added ice cubes from the refrigerator. The first drawer she opened contained white oversized wraparound aprons like the one Lars wore, and she took one and dunked it into the kettle.

Again she knelt beside him and had started to squeeze the cold water from the apron when he seized it from her and wrapped it, dripping wet, around his rapidly blistering leg. He caught his breath, but then let it out in a sigh of relief and spoke again. "There's a bathroom off the laundry." He waved in the general direction. "Bring me the first aid kit from the cabinet."

By the time she got back to the kitchen, he'd gotten off the floor and was sitting on a wooden chair, once more wrapping the cold, sopping apron around his leg. Wordlessly she handed him the white metal kit and a thick bath towel. He uttered a grunt that could have been either a terse thank-you or, more likely, a dismissal.

She decided to think of it as a thank-you and asked if she could help.

"Yes," he snapped. "Go back into the other part of the house and give me a little privacy. I don't need no fancy broad takin' care of me."

Mary Beth was more mystified than offended. Why was Flynn's houseman so antagonistic toward her? They'd only just met, yet she'd sensed his dislike even before the accident.

"I'm sure you don't," she said, and her tone was caustic, "but I'm not going to take any chances on your slipping again or collapsing. You'd either maim yourself or burn the house down, so you're stuck with me until Flynn comes back and hauls you off to the hospital, whether you like it or not."

She whirled away from the startled man and opened a door that looked as though it might be a broom closet. It was, and she took out a mop and began mopping up the water on the floor.

"Put that mop down," Lars commanded, and swore heartily. "I'll do that after I've taken care of this leg."

Mary Beth winced at the crudity of his adjectives. "Look," she snapped, "calling me a broad doesn't make me one, and I don't like your language. Either clean it up or keep quiet. You're not going to get rid of me by talking offensively, but you just might get the business end of this mop shoved down your throat."

If she hadn't been so angry, she'd have laughed at the look on his face. Apparently he had her pegged as being in training for sainthood, the way so many people did when they learned that her parents had been missionaries.

Flynn was almost certain to have told him about her background. Was that what he didn't like about her? Well, if he was around her for any length of time, he'd soon find that she seldom turned the other cheek.

Silence reigned for a while as she continued to mop and he carefully applied medication to his burns, then loosely bandaged them. When she'd finished, she took the mop outside.

Back in the kitchen, Lars was standing at the stove stirring something. He looked at her and muttered, "You'd better take your clothes off and run them through the dryer. You look like Cinderella before her fairy godmother got ahold of her."

Mary Beth looked down and realized that she was soaking wet and probably did look like a scullery maid. "But I don't have anything else to put on."

"The boss has got robes," he said. "Wrap one of them around you. No need to worry about seducing me—I'm immune."

Her sympathy for this disagreeable man was rapidly turning to dislike. "I wonder why that doesn't surprise me," she replied, and walked out of the kitchen.

She found the master bedroom upstairs. Like the rest of the house, it had an austere, strictly masculine decor. Nothing in it had come from their home in Baltimore. It was a corner room, with big windows that flooded the area with enough light to accentuate the heavy dark Spanish-style furniture. The wide bed was covered with a handwoven turquoise spread that was so beautiful in its detail that it doubled as a piece of Indian artwork.

Aware that she was starting to chill, Mary Beth quickly selected a royal-blue silk robe from Flynn's closet and headed for the bathroom. A hot shower banished the chill, and after drying off with a thick towel, she put on the robe and belted it around her slender waist. It would have come to just below the knee on Flynn, but on her it reached to the ankle.

A glance in the mirror showed that all the activity, plus the steam from the shower, had pretty well tousled her hairdo, and she unbraided it and ran a brush through it.

In the kitchen Lars didn't even turn to look at her when she padded across the damp floor in her bare feet to get to the laundry. She heard him limping around as she shoved her dress and underwear into the machine and turned it on, and her conscience wouldn't allow her to leave him to finish cooking dinner alone while suffering second- or third-degree burns. He might not want her help, but he was darn well going to get it.

She had misgivings about her state of undress, but decided that if it didn't bother him, why should it bother her? If she remembered to keep the robe pulled tightly around her, she'd be well covered even though she was nude underneath it.

"Why don't you let me do that?" she said, rolling up her sleeves as she came up behind where he stood peeling potatoes.

He looked at her with what could easily pass for contempt. "Because it's my job and my kitchen, and I don't want you here. Why don't you go back upstairs and think up new ways to torment the doc?"

Before she could react to the puzzling question, he swayed and dropped the peeler as he clutched the front of the sink.

"Lars!" Mary Beth reached for his arm in an effort to steady him, and it was like grabbing at solid rock.

He lowered his head between his massive shoulders and widened his stance to better support himself. "I'm okay, just a little dizzy," he insisted.

"You're not okay and you know it," she snapped. "Now stop being so darn obstinate. A severe burn can shock your whole system. You're built like a block of marble, and if you lose consciousness, there's no way I could either ease your fall or pick you up." She reached for the chair he'd been sitting in earlier and pulled it closer. "Now sit down and quit being such a pain or I'm going to call am ambulance."

This time he didn't argue, and instead sank onto the chair and sighed wearily.

Mary Beth picked up the peeler and the potato he'd been working on and prayed that Flynn would be home soon. For a few minutes she worked in silence, but then she heard Lars stir and glanced over to see him trying to stand.

"Lars, don't do that. If you want something, I'll get it for you."

He glared at her but did as she said. "Bring me the bottle of whiskey from the cupboard over there," he said gruffly.

She frowned. "If I remember my first aid correctly, that's not a good idea. Let me bring you a glass of ice water instead." She ran the cold water and started looking for a glass.

"If I'd wanted ice water, I'd have asked for it," he grumbled as she handed him the drink.

"Just humor me until Flynn comes. There must be something for pain in that kit I handed you."

She rummaged in the metal box and found what she was looking for. After reading the directions on the bottle, she poured two tablets into her palm and handed them to Lars.

He grumbled, but swallowed them and washed them down with the water. His sudden compliance was more distressing than his resistance. It indicated that he was in worse shape than he'd admit.

"Why don't you lie down for a while?" she asked. "I can help you to your bedroom."

"I'm not gonna pass out on you," he said scornfully. "Look at this." He raised one arm to flex it. The muscles bulged and rippled. "Not bad for an old guy, is it?" He flexed them again.

"Very impressive," she said, "and don't try to fool me, you're not all that old."

A fleeting impression of a smile touched the corners of his mouth. "The hell I'm not. I got a teenage grandson."

Mary Beth was truly surprised. It wasn't that he looked young, but neither did he look that old. "No! I find that hard to believe."

She meant it as a compliment, but he scowled. "Whatsa matter, you figure no woman would ever let me get close enough to her to give me a family?"

"That's not what I meant and you know it," she said. "You're being deliberately obnoxious. Why do you dislike me so?"

"What's to dislike?" he growled. "I don't even know you."

"Exactly my point. You don't know me, so why are you so belligerent?"

He shrugged. "All you have to do is tell the boss that I hurt your feelings and he'll kick me out. You got him twisted around your little finger."

She turned away and ran a small amount of water into the kettle of peeled potatoes. "I don't have Flynn twisted around my little finger, but if I did, it wouldn't be any of your business. What's the matter? Are you jealous of my relationship with him?"

His head snapped up, and he glared at her. "Just what in hell are you suggesting?"

She shook her head. "I'm not suggesting anything. Flynn made it plain that you were a friend who happened to work for him, not a casual employee, so I can't help wondering if you're afraid I'll interfere in some way with your friendship."

Lars's face twisted in a bitter grimace. "Look, lady, there's nothin' I'd like more than to see Doc settled down with a nice gal who would make him happy, but you're sure not her. He's been miserable over you ever since I've known him, and nothing's changed since you came back. As I see it, you're a selfish little tease who blows hot and cold and keeps him so worked up that he can't even look for another woman. The least you could do is set him free."

Mary Beth's eyes widened with anger. Why was it that she was always cast as the villain in the breakup of her marriage? She wasn't the one who'd been in love with someone else.

"So that's the way you see it, huh?" Her voice was thick with sarcasm. "Well, you'd better look again, because you've got it all wrong. And what do you mean I should set him free? We've been divorced for three years—how much freer can he get?"

Lars looked stunned. "Divorced? Doc never mentioned no divorce."

She slumped with despair. "Yes, I've noticed. It does tend to slip his mind frequently. Or rather I should say he simply ignores it."

She noticed that Lars was rubbing his face with both hands and looking as if he'd reached the end of his endurance. Quickly she carried the kettle of potatoes to the stove and turned the heat on low.

"Come on, Lars," she said as she walked back toward him. "Let's get you to your room and into bed while you can still get around. I suspect those pills I gave you were pretty strong."

She put out her hands and helped him to stand, and he tottered and clutched her around the shoulders. Slipping her arm around his waist to steady him, she asked, "Where's your room?"

"Next to the bathroom." His words were beginning to slur, and he kept his arm around her shoulders as she helped him across the kitchen.

They were almost to the laundry when the kitchen door swung open and shut behind them, and Flynn's voice, filled with outrage, boomed in the silence.

"What in hell is going on here!"

Chapter Nine

Mary Beth was puzzled by Flynn's tone, but relieved that he was home as she turned her head to look at him. the relief vanished when she saw his stormy expression.

For a moment she was at a loss to understand why he was so angry, but a glance at Lars, then down at herself, solved the puzzle. She was wearing nothing but Flynn's robe, which Lars's heavy arm had displaced so that it gaped across the bosom. The retired wrestler's pants were ripped almost to the hip, the rest of his clothes were disheveled, and they were walking toward the bedroom with their arms around each other!

A wave of guilt swept over her even though she had nothing to feel guilty about, and her own temper bristled. Flynn knew her well enough to know that no matter how it looked, she'd never behave in the manner he was imagining.

Before she could answer, Lars stumbled, and she cried out as his weight threatened to throw her off balance, too.

Immediately Flynn was across the room and grasped Lars from the other side. "Good Lord, what's happened?" he asked as he took the brunt of the heavy man's weight.

They balanced Lars between them and continued toward the bedroom. "He spilled hot water on his leg and it's badly burned." Mary Beth explained. "The idiot wouldn't let me call an ambulance, so I gave him some of the pills for pain from the first aid kit. He was doing all right until a few minutes ago when he started getting lightheaded. I don't know whether it's from delayed shock or the medicine."

Flynn glanced down at Lars's bandaged leg. "Probably a little of both," he muttered in a tone that betrayed both anxiety and impatience. "Now suppose you tell me why you're running around with no clothes on."

She gave him a scathing glance. "Because I got sopping wet cavorting about on the floor in the water, trying to help this big stubborn lug. Not that I got any thanks for it," she muttered as an afterthought. "My clothes are in the dryer."

In the bedroom they deposited their burden on the bed. "Call 911 and tell them to send an ambulance," Flynn said.

Lars raised up on his elbows and bellowed. "I'm not goin' to no hospital! Come on, Doc, I got a hide like an alligator—a little hot water's not gonna do much damage. It's those damn pills this gal of yours gave me that's makin' me dizzy." He glared at Mary Beth. "I told ya' I wanted whiskey."

She stood by the bed uncertainly, wondering which strong-willed man she should obey. It seemed doubtful that Lars would allow the medics to treat him even if they came.

Flynn must have decided the same thing, because he sighed with exasperation and sat down on the side of the bed. "Bring me that first aid kit, Mary Beth."

He glanced pointedly at Lars. "I'll take a look at your leg, but if I feel it should be treated at the hospital, then that's where you're going even if I have to take you there in a straitjacket."

She brought the kit, and when Flynn asked her to step out of the room while he examined his patient, she returned to the kitchen to check on the neglected dinner preparations. Surprisingly, everything was coming along very well.

Vaguely remembering that the table had already been set when she'd gone through the dining room earlier, she went in to make sure. It was, and it looked exquisite. The table was covered with a dark brown linen cloth, and the centerpiece was another arrangement of Thanksgiving flowers, this time in a silver bowl. Yellow candles gleamed in silver candlesticks.

As she walked closer, her heart seemed to do a flip-flop. The place settings were pieces of the Waterford crystal, Lennox china and Wallace sterling that Flynn's parents had given them for a wedding present. Joan had asked her to pick the patterns, and the beautiful settings had been very special to her. She'd used them often and they represented many happy times.

She picked up one of the plates and ran her fingertips over the salmon-pink flower design, then around the delicate gold border at the edge. She wasn't aware that she was crying until a single tear fell on the translucent china. Then with a sob she clasped the plate to her breast and let the tears flow.

She wasn't sure how long she stood there before she heard the kitchen door swing open and Flynn's voice calling to her. "Mary Beth. Oh, there you are."

Startled, she swung around to face him.

"I've decided to..." he said, then stopped talking and hurried to her as he scanned her face anxiously. "You're crying. What's the matter?"

She held out the plate to him in a gesture of supplication. "You...you kept our wedding gifts."

He took the plate and set it on the table beside them, then cupped her face with his hands. "Of course I kept the things that meant so much to you. They were all I had left besides memories."

With his thumbs he gently brushed at the tears on her cheeks, then lowered his head and kissed her closed eyelids and licked the salty moisture that still trickled from underneath. "I have all of our things in storage waiting for you."

He put his arms around her and drew her close, and she snuggled into his embrace. "Flynn," she whispered brokenly, "I have to know. Why didn't you marry Vanessa?"

He caressed her temple with his lips. "Because I'm in love with you," he answered simply.

Her breath caught, and her heart skipped a beat as she looked up at him. "But why...?"

He kissed her lightly, stilling her. "Not now. Later tonight I promise we'll have a long talk, but right now there's Lars to see to. I've dressed his leg properly, and he's right, he is a tough old bird. The burns are painful but not as serious as I'd first thought, so I'm not going to insist that he go to the hospital."

Flynn chuckled. "He's determined to keep the Thanksgiving dinner date with his lady friend. He called to tell her what happened, and she's invited him to spend the next few days with her so she can look after him. She'll be here in a few minutes to pick him up."

Mary Beth sniffed with disbelief. "I wish the poor lady luck. If she thinks she's going to take care of Lars, she's going to need it. That man is impossible!"

Flynn grinned. "I agree, but wait until you see Bella. She's a lady wrestler, and I think she can handle him."

Somehow without her realizing it, he'd untied the sash that held her robe closed, and when he repositioned his arms underneath it to clasp her nude body, she shivered with desire.

"Flynn, you mustn't," she murmured uselessly since they both knew that he must.

"Oh, sweetheart," he said brokenly as his hands explored her bareness, "have you any idea how many times in the last three years I've longed to hold you like this? It's been an almost constant torment."

She only wished he was as nude as she was as she stroked his back and moved restlessly against him. "It couldn't be any more often than I've longed for you," she whispered, then gasped as his roaming hands found her breasts.

It was so familiar, and so right, and all of her misgivings dissolved as the heat of passion melded them together.

Flynn struggled valiantly to hang on to some semblance of control as he held his nude wife in his hungry arms. Dear God, he should never have touched her, but it had been so long and he'd known that she wore nothing under that robe. He was only human, and he needed her so badly.

He sucked in his breath and joined her in the rhythmic movements that were driving him crazy. He couldn't stop now, but neither could he take her on the nearest couch like a teenager. He was thirty-seven years old; surely he could dredge up enough dignity to at least wait until there was no one else in the house.

The doorbell rang, and the shock to his system was almost his undoing as reality finally gave him the strength he needed to put Mary Beth away from him. She looked dazed, and for a moment he almost pulled her back into his embrace, but the bell rang again and finally broke the spell.

"For the sake of my sanity, love, put your clothes on," he muttered huskily just before he strode to the door to admit the lady wrestler.

Two hours later things had finally quieted down. Lars and Bella were gone, Mary Beth had dressed except for her panty hose that couldn't be put in the dryer and were still damp, and Flynn had helped her put the finishing touches on the delayed Thanksgiving dinner. They'd dined leisurely together by candlelight.

A clock somewhere in the house chimed seven as they settled down on the sofa in front of the fireplace in the living room with their pie and coffee.

"I don't know when I've had a more delicious meal," she said. "Lars really is a marvelous cook. I'm so sorry he got burned. Are you sure he'll be okay?"

Flynn swallowed a bite of pie. "He should be if he and Bella don't get too...uh...active. Bella can handle him if anyone can, so I'm not worried."

Mary Beth chuckled as the image of the lady Amazon with red hair and muscles almost as big as Lars's came to mind. "You may be right," she said, then sobered. "He told me that he has a grandson. So he must have children."

"One," Flynn said, "a daughter. He was married when he was quite young, but apparently his wife decided he was too rough and uncouth for her taste. She left him when their little girl was five and took the child half a continent away. She later married a school teacher, and Lars didn't see his daughter again until she was grown and looked him up."

Flynn put his empty plate on the coffee table. "He worships her and his grandson, but they're really not a part of his life. They still live in the Midwest where her mother and stepfather are, and Lars only sees them the few times they've been able to come out here for a visit."

Mary Beth shook her head. "That's sad. No wonder he doesn't like women, if his wife treated him so shabbily."

Flynn raised one eyebrow. "What do you mean? Lars is an enthusiastic womanizer. You'd be surprised at the following those muscles attract."

"Then it's just me he doesn't like," she mused aloud.

Flynn's amusement vanished. "Why do you say that? Did he mistreat you in some way while I was gone?" His tone was harsh.

She could have bitten her tongue. "No, of course not," she said not altogether truthfully. "But he did growl a bit and tell me he could take care of himself. I got the idea he wasn't exactly pining for my company."

"Mary Beth, if he did or said anything to upset you, I want to know it. I won't put up with—"

"Flynn, it's all right," She interrupted as she put her hand on his arm. "He was in a great deal of pain, and I do have a tendency to hover in such cases, much to his disgust."

Flynn put his arm around her and pulled her to his side. "Don't waste your time on the ungrateful brute," he said. "You can hover over me anytime."

The stirring of desire that had only been tempered came to life under his endearing words and the brush of his hand across her breast. "The next time I get the urge to hover, I'll come looking for you," she said with a smile.

He caressed her forehead with his lips. "All you have to do is reach out, I'll be there."

Those words were reassuring, but when she'd reached out to him while they were married, there'd been another woman in his arms. That was a long time ago, and she knew he was no longer involved with Vanessa, but still the hurt and humiliation of knowing he'd only stayed married to her out of a misplaced sense of duty wouldn't go away.

They could never be happy until the issue had been brought out and discussed openly and honestly.

Regretfully she pulled away from him and sat up. "Flynn, you said we'd talk later about why you didn't marry Vanessa. We can't put it off any longer."

The satisfied look he'd worn minutes earlier vanished, replaced by anxiety. "You're right. I tried to explain my feelings before you filed for divorce, but you wouldn't listen. Then you ran away and I couldn't."

"I didn't run away."

"Yes, you did. You disappeared instead of staying and trying to work things out. I'm not accusing you, darling. You were young and unsophisticated, and I've always admitted I was in the wrong, but you did run from the problem. Now, what is it you want to know?"

Deep down she knew he was right, but she wasn't yet willing to admit it. Instead she answered his question. "Why did you stay with me when you were in love with Vanessa?"

He sighed wearily. "It's true, I was in love with her, or thought I was, when I married you. We'd started dating in our second year of medical school and became engaged the Christmas before graduation. We were both looking forward to a wedding when I'd fulfilled my obligation in Central America. My only intention when I married you was to get you out of that war-torn country and back to the United States."

His words were like whips biting into her tender flesh, but she had to continue. "Then why didn't you tell me that and have the marriage annulled immediately?"

He moved his hands in a gesture of dismissal. "You know why. We've been over this time after time. There was no one to take care of you."

"Why didn't you get in touch with the missionary board? They'd have made sure I was looked after."

"Because I wanted you with me, and don't ask me why. I still thought I was in love with Vanessa and she was furious, my parents were upset, and I felt like a heel, but you treated me like a cross between a hero and a savior. You were so sweet, and so loving, and the very mention of sending you away made me sick to my stomach. I was too damn stupid to realize that it was you I was in love with, but when we finally consummated the marriage, I knew I'd never let you go."

Mary Beth could have screamed with frustration. "Darn it, Flynn, you keep saying that, but I find it hard to believe when I saw you kissing your ex-fiancé."

Flynn stood and walked to the fireplace, where he looked down at the crackling flames. "The feelings were all on her side. I didn't want to hurt her by not responding."

Mary Beth flinched. "Oh, come on, Flynn, I'm not the naive girl I was then."

He shook his head, but didn't turn to look at her. "I know, that's the classic line for a guy caught with another woman, but in my case it happens to be true. When I first took you to Baltimore with me, I assured Van that there was nothing between us and I'd get an annulment as soon as you'd had a chance to recover from the grief over your parents' shocking deaths.''

He moved away from the fire and started pacing. ''After we started sleeping together, I tried to tell her that things had changed between us, but she got the idea that I meant to wait until you'd finished school and then divorce you. That was not my intention and I told her so, but I felt so damn guilty that I'm afraid I didn't stress it forcefully enough. Since she lived so far away, I figured she'd find another man and forget about me.''

He stopped his pacing and stood looking down at her. ''I don't know how to explain my feelings to you, Mary Beth. I admit that even though I wanted you, I never fully committed myself to you during the time we were together. I was wrong. Tragically, as it turned out, but I had this small, nagging sense of being manipulated—not by you,'' he hurried to explain when she gasped. ''By fate, circumstances, whatever. I was torn between my raging passion for you and my sense of duty toward Van.''

Mary Beth closed her eyes so he wouldn't see the pain she couldn't disguise. ''So you only stayed with me because I was good in bed,'' she murmured unhappily.

Flynn hunkered down in front of her and took both her hands in his. ''Sweetheart, you're not listening to me, or maybe I'm just doing this badly.'' His expressive features were twisted with anxiety. ''I stayed with you because I loved you so deeply that I couldn't imagine life without you, but I was too perverse and stubborn to admit it. The seed of resentment that I hadn't gotten the woman I thought I'd wanted nagged at me just enough to keep me from realizing how truly blessed I really was.''

He kissed the palms of each of her hands, then buried his face in them. "The situation that night when you came home and found Vanessa and me in an embrace wasn't at all what you thought. You'd been in Falls Church, baby-sitting Carol's children for a couple of days while she was in the hospital after an emergency appendectomy, and I was eagerly looking forward to your return home the following day. I'd arrived back at the house late that evening, and when the doorbell rang, I'd thought it was Mom stopping by to see how I was getting along."

He kissed her palms again, then raised his head. "It was Vanessa. I was surprised, because she'd never been to our house before. I hadn't even known she was in town, but I invited her in and took her back to the den where I'd been reading. We chatted for a while, and then she began to reminisce about our days in med school."

He scowled, then released her hands and stood again. "Hell, honey, I don't even know how it happened. She was coming on to me, and I was trying to fend her off without hurting her feelings...."

With a muttered oath he turned away and ran his fingers through his light brown hair. "Damn, I sound like an innocent virgin telling about being attacked by the town siren," he said with disgust, "but I swear that's the way it was. By then she had me feeling guilty again for practically abandoning her at the altar, as she put it. It got to the point where I either had to kiss her or beat her off with a stick. The kiss didn't mean anything to me, but the other alternative seemed a little extreme so I kissed her. That's what was happening when you opened the door."

Mary Beth had to admit that what he said could be true. Shocked though she'd been at the time, she'd noticed that both of them were fully dressed. Now that she thought back, she realized that they hadn't even been disheveled.

She felt as if the warm sun had finally come out after a long, frozen winter.

"I can accept that," she said slowly, "but I still don't understand why you didn't marry Vanessa after I left. You've admitted that you still had feelings for her."

"Feelings, sure," he answered. "Regret at having treated her so badly, pity for the hurt I'd caused her, guilt in abundance, but not love. In that instant when I looked up and saw you standing in the doorway looking so shattered, I knew that you were the only woman I ever had, or would, love."

He turned around slowly, and his gaze found and held hers. "I also knew I'd probably lost you forever, and the anguish was unbearable. After that I couldn't stand the sight of Vanessa, and I never had any contact with her again."

The chilling torment of rejection and humiliation that Mary Beth had carried with her for three years was finally receding, fading with her recognition of the truth. She could see the honesty in his face and feel it in the magnetism that radiated between them.

Slowly she rose and stood before him. Putting out her hand, she caressed his cheek as she raised her face to his. When she spoke, her voice shook. "Can you ever forgive me for being such a selfish, immature child? You're right, I did run away. I told myself that I was doing it for you, so you wouldn't feel responsible for me, but I know now that it was only my own feelings I was concerned with. I didn't care how worried you'd be, or how guilty you'd feel. I was running away from my own pain and not giving a thought to yours."

While she was speaking, he put his arms around her and held her close. "You could never be selfish, my darling, and I was fascinated by the child in you. My biggest regret is that I seem to have destroyed her, but I got a warm and loving woman in return. I love you, Mary Beth."

She clasped him around the neck as his mouth covered hers, gently at first as if afraid she might object, then with more pressure as one hand moved to caress the firm curve of her derriere while the other found her breast.

Her lips parted to admit his invading tongue, and she trembled with the onslaught of heat the familiar probing unleashed. A gentle push on her bottom brought her into intimate contact with the heat in his own loins, and she moaned softly as the tautness between them escalated into a throbbing turbulence.

When his hand settled on her bare thigh, she couldn't stifle a cry of pleasure from deep in her being. For a moment his fingers dug into her overheated flesh in what she recognized as an effort on his part to keep his own control, then moved slowly upward.

"Oh, Flynn, please..." She wasn't sure whether she was pleading with him to stop or escalate, but they both knew that stopping wasn't an option as he swept her up into his arms and walked across the room with her.

Upstairs he switched on the light in his bedroom and stood her down beside the bed while he pulled back the covers. "Lie down, sweetheart," he said, and pulled his sweater and knit shirt over his head.

The short journey had restored a small portion of her nagging conscience, and she hesitated. What she was about to do was irreversible. She couldn't make love with him now and not commit herself to him totally. It was true they'd overcome the obstacle of her misunderstanding, but there was still the problem of his domination.

"Flynn, I... I don't think..." Her tone betrayed her need for him in spite of her words.

He studied her carefully for a moment, then put his hands at her waist. "It's all right, sweetheart. We won't do anything you don't want to do, but lie here with me and let me hold you, kiss you, caress you."

Her knees literally gave way, and he lowered her to the bed, then took off his shoes and socks and lay down beside her. The mattress seemed to fit itself to her curves, and the down-filled pillow held her head in a buoyant softness.

He turned on his side and took her in his arms, and she snuggled against his bare masculine chest. Her joy at lying with him in bed again was almost uncontainable. She loved him so much, and three years of nights between cold lonely sheets without him banished her fleeting doubts.

She raised her face for his kiss, but instead of taking her mouth, he brushed his lips across her forehead, down her cheek, and under her silky hair to nuzzle the pounding pulse at the side of her throat.

"I love you," he whispered as one hand settled on her bent knee and trailed slowly up the outside curve of her thigh.

"I love you, too," she whispered in answer, and let her palm roam over his broad muscular back. "I've been so miserable without you. I've never wanted any other man."

He tensed and raised his head, and she could see the cautious expression on his face only inches away. "Not even Don MacGregor?" His tone was raspy.

She'd been angry when he'd asked before if she was sleeping with Don, and had refused to tell him. Now she could see how important the answer was to him, and she happily set his mind at ease.

"Not even Don," she said.

The lines of anxiety on his brow smoothed as he exhaled the breath he'd been holding. "You can't possibly know what a relief that is to me."

His roaming hand moved across her silk panties and up to her waist. "Let me take off your dress," he pleaded. "I want to see you. To feel you the way you were under my robe earlier."

She knew that wasn't a good idea. They both had all the stimulation they could handle, but the heat of the memory of those few minutes in the dining room melted her good intentions, and when her dress came off, her bra went with it. She wasn't sure which of them unfastened it.

"Oh, you feel so good," he said with a drawn-out sigh.

He pressed her to him with one hand while the other cupped her nude breast. "You're fuller than you used to be," he observed as he took her throbbing nipple in his mouth.

His suckling intensified the restless fire deep in her womanhood, and she clutched at his hips in an effort to pull him closer. His male rigidity pressing against her lower abdomen scattered her wits, and in an involuntary movement she put one leg across both of his and rolled over so she was lying on top of him.

The rough wool of his slacks was an intrusion, but when he put his hand between them to unfasten the button and zipper, a small shock jolted her.

She shouldn't be doing this!

Moving her hand over his to still it, she almost sobbed. "Flynn, it's wrong...."

For a moment he tensed, then he put his arms around her and held her head against his pounding heart. "No, Mary Beth, it's not wrong," he said gently, although the tension in him betrayed the effort his patience was costing. "It's very right. You're my wife. You have been ever since we took our vows, and you always will be. We belong together, and we need each other so badly. Love me, sweetheart, and let me love you.''

How could she argue with that? Surely he was right. The vows they'd taken were meant to be forever. The divorce was just a legal formality. If they loved each other, it couldn't be wrong to express that love.

She raised her head and looked down into his anxiety-clouded eyes. ''It never used to take you so long to get out of your pants,'' she said huskily.

With a shout of amusement and relief, he rolled them over so that he was on top. ''Time me,'' he said exuberantly. ''I'm going to beat my old record.''

She watched him as he quickly got out of bed and removed his slacks and briefs. His body was every bit as beautiful as she'd remembered, and she held out her eager arms to him. ''You're wearing white briefs,'' she murmured happily as she snuggled once more in his embrace. ''Didn't you like the colored ones I bought you?''

His impatient hands sought her most sensitive places. ''They wore out,'' he said, and nibbled on her earlobe. ''I just replaced them with white. After all, there was no one to see or care what color they were.''

A thrill that was apart from what he was doing to her with his fingers ran through her, and this time when she spoke, there was no teasing in her tone. ''Flynn, are you telling me that you...'' She paused, finding it hard to voice her suspicion.

He did it for her. ''Yes, love, I'm telling you that I've been as celibate as you have for the past three years. I couldn't sleep with another woman when I was in love with you.''

For one of the first times in her life, Mary Beth was speechless. The joy that welled in her was too overwhelming to express, but as she opened herself to him, she silently vowed that his faithfulness would be rewarded. She'd give him a night that would show him how grateful she was even if she couldn't put it into words.

At dawn they finally went to sleep for the last time, and when Mary Beth woke just before noon, Flynn was still dozing. It seemed like all the other mornings when she'd wakened beside him, but a persistent doubt buried in her bothersome conscience reminded her that it wasn't. They'd been married before, but now they weren't.

She'd been too aroused last night to argue with his reasoning on the subject, but now that she was replete and sated, her strict upbringing was making her pay. Not that the physical act of loving Flynn was wrong, she could never believe that, but making love without a commitment could leave her vulnerable.

Not once in their long night of loving had Flynn asked her to marry him again. He'd been alternately fierce and gentle, giving and taking, masterful and submissive, but even though he'd told her time and again that he loved her, needed her, he hadn't mentioned marriage.

She shifted restlessly in his embrace, and his arms tightened around her. "Don't get up," he said as he nuzzled her throat. "I think I'm good for one more go-around."

For some reason his assumption that she was his to do with as he pleased annoyed her, but she tried not to show it. Instead she turned and kissed him. "Flynn, you're insatiable," she teased.

"Honey, it's been a long, long time," he muttered, and cupped her breast.

As always she responded immediately, but perversely she didn't want to be aroused. "I'm hungry," she said for want of a better excuse. "It's lunchtime."

He chuckled. "How could I have forgotten about that ravenous appetite of yours? I can see that my grocery bill will go sky-high now that we'll be living together again."

The statement that should have thrilled her brought a chill instead, and she pulled out of his arms and sat up. "Flynn, I don't want to repeat my past mistakes this time, so tell me what it is you want of me. Are you suggesting that I live here with you as your mistress?"

For a moment his expression was blank, then changed to shocked disbelief as he, too, sat up. "My mistress? For God's sake, whatever gave you that idea?"

She ran her hand through her long disheveled hair. "What else could I think? You haven't said anything about getting married again."

He blinked with astonishment. "But I told you..."

He stopped and studied her intently, then swung his feet off the bed and stood. "Mary Beth, I thought you understood what I told you last night," he said as he pulled on his pants. "We don't have to repeat our vows—we're still married."

She gasped with impatience. What on earth was the matter with him? She'd never known him to be irrational before. "Darn it, Flynn, don't start that again," she snapped as she, too, slid out of bed and started dressing. "I filed for divorce before I left for Spain. We sat down with our lawyers and agreed to a settlement—"

"Which you never had any intention of accepting," he interrupted. "You left without taking any of the things I'd agreed you should have."

"That doesn't cancel out the fact that you agreed to the divorce and the papers were filed," she said as she pulled her dress over her head.

"I never agreed to the divorce," he argued. "I only went along with it to give you a chance to calm down a little. I had no intention of letting you leave me."

"*Letting* me leave you?" There was a cutting edge to her tone. "You didn't have anything to say about whether or not I left you."

He'd finished dressing and came around the bed to stand in front of her. "Yes, I did, sweetheart," he said gently, "and you made it easy for me by not showing up for the court hearing. I asked that the action be set aside since you were unavailable. The judge agreed."

He reached out and cupped her shoulders. "Mary Beth, the divorce was never granted. You've always been my wife."

She could only stare at him as her smoldering emotions escalated from disbelief to outrage. Then her control shattered, and her voice was low and taut when she finally spoke.

"You arrogant bastard!"

The words seemed to echo and reecho throughout the room.

Chapter Ten

Mary Beth jerked away from Flynn and put several feet of distance between them.

"How dare you meddle with my life! How dare you!" She was so angry that she couldn't even express herself except in timeworn clichés.

The blood drained from his face. "I wasn't meddling." His tone was calm, reasonable. "You were still my wife and you'd disappeared without a trace. That's hardly the action of a rational person. I was going out of my mind with worry."

She wasn't buying it. "Nonsense. I knew exactly what I was doing. I was twenty-one years old and a college graduate. You had no right to make decisions for me. Decisions that could have been disastrous." She put her hands to her face as a thought occurred to her. "Dear Lord, what if I'd married again and had children without ever knowing I wasn't free?"

Flynn started toward her, but she backed away. "Don't come near me," she grated.

Anxiety clouded his features, but when he spoke he did so quietly. "Mary Beth, I didn't for a minute believe that you weren't in touch with your lawyer. That's one of the reasons I did it. I'd hoped it would bring you out of hiding. All the time you were gone, I thought you knew about the action and didn't contest it."

"Your inflated ego is disgusting," she snapped. "What made you think I'd meekly sit by and let you get away with a thing like that if I'd known about it?"

"I hoped you loved me enough to come back and try to work things out once you'd had a chance to think it through."

"Oh, I loved you," she said self-disparagingly. "There was never any doubt about that, was there? I feel humiliated every time I think of what a lovesick little goose I was. I even continued to let you dictate my every move long after I'd learned to think for myself, because I didn't want to displease you."

He ran his fingers through his hair. "Why were you so sure I'd be displeased that you were becoming more independent? I always knew you'd grow up someday. I can see where I might have seemed to be bossy, even possessive, but in the beginning your very life had depended on my making the decisions. You seemed happy with that arrangement, and I'm not a mind reader. If you didn't like it, you should have said so."

Mary Beth's innate honesty demanded that she recognize the truth of his statement, but she was too furious to admit it to him. "I'm telling you now and have been ever since I came back, but it doesn't do any good. It was bad enough when you had me watched by a private detective, and now you tell me that all this time you've known I thought we were divorced and you didn't bother to mention that we aren't."

The more she thought of it the madder she became. Without bothering to get her panty hose off the shower curtain rod, she stepped into her pumps and started out of the room.

With a muttered oath, Flynn caught up and they bounced down the stairs together. "If you'll stay in one place for a minute, I'll explain why I didn't tell you," he said, exasperated.

she spied her purse beside the sofa and picked it up. "Don't bother," she snapped as she headed for the door. "I wouldn't believe you anyway."

This time he caught her up by the arm and whirled her around. His anxiety had changed to pure rage. "I have something to say to you, Mary Elizabeth, and you're not leaving here until you hear it."

He clasped her by both arms and held her still. His expression warned her that she'd better be quiet and listen.

She glared at him, but he didn't seem to notice or care. "I'm sick to death of groveling." His voice was laced with steel. "I'm not going to do it any longer. I've made lots of mistakes, but I've admitted them. I was wrong to have allowed Vanessa to think she and I might someday have a future together. I was wrong to hire a security guard without your permission, and I should have told you as soon as you returned that we were still married. Those were mistakes, and I've paid dearly for them and tried to make amends, but you're not going to give an inch."

His fingers were digging into her arms, but when she moved them to try to loosen his hold, he seemed to assume she was trying to get away, and tightened it instead.

"You're not in love with me," he continued. "All you're interested in now is your precious independence. Your freedom to do whatever you damn please and to hell with anyone else. You've changed, but don't kid yourself that you've grown up. You're still running away from your problems."

She gasped with indignation and again tried to pull away from him, but he wouldn't let her go. "You've been awfully free with your accusations, but you won't take the time to listen to my explanations. Okay, if that's the way you want it, I won't stop you, but if you walk out on me now, don't expect me to follow and coax you to come back."

There was a frightening finality in his words, and though he released her, she didn't move as he spoke again.

"You've finally gotten through to me, Mary Beth." He no longer sounded angry, just tired. "I won't make any demands on you. You're free to leave, and I won't interfere if you want to seek a dissolution of our marriage. I'll give you whatever you want, but you'll have to ask. I'm no longer offering anything."

She saw by his tight, closed expression that he meant every word. Panic swept through her, but she managed to maintain her self-control. He was only giving her what she wanted—her independence and freedom. She'd finally won.

Taking a deep breath, she turned around and walked out the door, closing it softly behind her.

As she drove away, she wondered why winning was such a mockery, why it felt so much like a crushing defeat.

Flynn stood in the entryway and listened to Mary Beth start her car and pull out of the driveway. He hadn't moved since she'd turned her back on him and left. He wasn't sure he could. His shoulders felt as if they'd just been fitted with weights, and his legs trembled.

With a massive effort he managed to pull himself together and walk to the kitchen where he got busy making coffee. How could anything as beautiful as the night he and Mary Beth had just shared have ended so disastrously?

He clutched at the back of his neck in a gesture of despair. That was a stupid question; he'd known it was going to happen when he told her what he'd done. Why wasn't he better prepared?

Maybe it was because they'd been so truly one just hours before. She'd been as eager as he, and had responded with the same abandon that he'd always treasured in her. Neither of them had held anything back in their desperate need for each other, and he'd honestly thought she'd understood when he'd told her she was still his wife.

His legs were still rubbery, and he pulled out a chair and sat down at the round oak table. Well, he'd really done it now. His hold on her had been tenuous at best; this time she'd never forgive or forget.

He'd meant what he said, though. He'd done all the apologizing he intended to do. If she'd didn't know by now how much he loved her, wanted her, then it was best to break off the relationship. He'd had all the mood swings he could stand. It was affecting his work, and as a physician he couldn't let that happen. Too often a child's life depended on his clear thinking and keen skill.

Not even for Mary Beth would he jeopardize his little patients.

No, it was better to let her go and try to get on with his own life. He'd made a grave error in requesting that the divorce action be withdrawn three years ago. This time he wouldn't contest it.

For two weeks Mary Beth existed in a state of conflicting emotions. She hated Flynn; she loved him. She wanted a divorce; she was glad they were still married. She wouldn't compromise her independence; she wanted him no matter what she had to give up.

The vacillating was driving her crazy, interfering with her concentration during the day and keeping her awake nights.

But indecision wasn't the only thing that threatened her with madness. The memory of their passionate night together was an almost constant torment. Her heart told her that no woman in her right mind would give up a man who made love to her as thoroughly and as erotically as Flynn did, but her mind remembered that he'd deceived her, not once but three different times. How could she live with a man she couldn't trust?

Her roommate, Peggy, with her usual tenacity had gotten the story of what had happened with Flynn out of Mary Beth, but instead of encouraging her in her outrage at his high-handed tactics, she'd scolded her thoroughly.

"Good Lord, woman," she'd sputtered, "what's the matter with you? Most of us would sell our souls for a man who'd love us as deeply and as passionately as Flynn has proven that he loves you, but you—you won't settle for less than Prince Charming, Lochinvar and Mr. Clean all rolled into one. Well, I've got news for you. Those characters never existed, and neither does the man you're looking for."

Mary Beth had been too astonished by the outburst to argue as Peg continued. "How come you're so perfect that you can't accept anything but perfection in a hus-

band? Seems to me it was pretty selfish of you to hang on
to Flynn when you knew he'd only married you to get you
out of Central America."

"But I didn't—"

"Oh, come on now, you're not stupid," she muttered.
"You knew he had a fiancée in the States, and I gather
he'd never made a pass at you or indicated that he was
attracted to you before your parents were killed."

A tiny suspicion that Mary Beth neither wanted nor
welcomed gnawed at her. "That's true, but—"

"He even told you when you got to Texas that his plan
was to leave you with relatives when he went on to Baltimore."

The suspicion turned to panic. "You're twisting everything," Mary Beth yelled in her effort to banish the un-
wanted truth. "That's not the way it was. You don't know
what happened. You weren't there."

Peggy shrugged. "That's true, but I'm just repeating
what you've told me. Are you saying you were lying?"

"Of course not. I never lie."

"Then just think about it. You can't have it both ways.
Personally, I don't believe you were as naive and innocent as you like to think you were. I think you knew that
Flynn's purpose in marrying you was just to get you out
of the country, but you were shocked and terrified at the
idea of being all alone in the United States. You were also
in love with him, and either consciously or subconsciously you were determined not to give him up."

Her gaze had caught and held Mary Beth's. "You
trapped him into a marriage that he didn't want, and in
my opinion you're damn lucky he stood still for it. I suggest that you take a good look at your own motives before you go pointing your finger at his."

At the time, Mary Beth had still been too angry with Flynn and too unnerved by Peggy's unjust accusations to do any objective thinking. She hadn't spoken to Peggy for two days after that, and their relationship was still strained and uncomfortable, but lately she'd begun having the nightmare again. Over and over, the dream replayed the incident that had broken up her marriage, and it forced her to reflect on what her friend had said.

The introspection was painful. She knew she hadn't deliberately held Flynn to their vows, but was it possible that she'd subconsciously played on his strong protective instincts?

By Friday of the first full week in December, her anguish was apparent in the paleness of her face, the blue circles under her eyes and the lines of exhaustion that spoke of her sleepless nights.

San Diego was in the grip of a rare cold spell, with overnight temperatures in the thirties. Not low enough to earn sympathy from states that were knee-deep in snow and ice, but the residents of Southern California weren't prepared for the chill. There were a lot of colds and flu-like illnesses, and they'd struck heavily in the schools, with a high absentee rate of both teachers and students.

On this Friday at least one-third of the pupils in Mary Beth's classes were absent, and some of the others were coughing and sniffling. One in particular, Juanita Messa, worried her. Juanita was usually cheerful and quick to participate, but today she'd been restless and withdrawn. Although she didn't appear to be ill, she was lethargic and her red swollen eyes looked as if she'd been crying.

At lunchtime Mary Beth took her aside and asked if there was something troubling her. Immediately the child burst into tears, and Mary Beth held her until the storm had passed.

"Now tell me what's the matter, honey," she said as she brushed the dark disheveled hair away from the pale little face.

"It's ... it's my baby sister," she stammered in her native Spanish. "She's so sick. She coughs so bad and she feels hot and she makes a funny noise when she breathes." Another sob shook her. "Oh, Miss Warren, I'm afraid she's going to die!"

"How old is she?" Mary Beth asked, also speaking in Spanish and trying not to let her own anxiety show.

"Almost a year old."

"Has your mother taken her to a doctor?"

Juanita shook her head. "No. Mama says she'll be all right, she doesn't need a doctor. But I'm so scared...."

So was Mary Beth. It sounded as though the child needed immediate medical attention. "Maybe I can help," she said reassuringly. "Come with me to the school nurse and we'll ask her to go to your home and examine the baby."

"No, we mustn't," Juanita cried. "Papa doesn't like doctors and nurses and hospitals. He says we'll take care of Theresa ourselves."

Mary Beth was puzzled. She was certain that this was not an abusive home. Juanita was much too happy and open, but for some reason her parents were taking dangerous chances with their younger child's health rather than seek medical help.

She knew it was useless to insist. Instead she tried another tactic. "Would you like me to go to your house and talk to your mama and papa?"

The little girl nodded, and Mary Beth arranged to drive her home at the end of the school day.

Three hours later they drove up to the small shabby house and went inside. The mother, a haggard, middle-aged woman, sat in a wooden chair, rocking a coughing child wrapped in a blanket.

Still speaking Spanish, Mary Beth introduced herself, explained why she was there and asked if she could see the baby. The woman loosened the blanket, and a spasm of coughing shook the small frame.

It was evident that the child was very ill. Aside from the racking cough, she radiated heat and her breathing was laborious.

"Mrs. Messa, Theresa needs to be seen by a doctor," she said, careful not to sound judgmental.

Tears welled in the woman's eyes. "We have no money for doctors," she said, also in Spanish.

A wave of pity shook Mary Beth, followed by an equally strong anger. Pity for the agony this mother was experiencing, and anger that a concentrated effort was obviously not made to acquaint non-English-speaking citizens with the rights they were entitled to.

"There are places where you can get medical care without money," she said. "I'll see to it for you, but we must get this little one to a hospital."

She jumped as a gruff voice spoke from behind her. "No hospital."

She stood and turned to see a dark husky man with a look of defeat on his lined face. Juanita called him "Papa."

Mary Beth introduced herself and again explained that there was free medical care available for his daughter, but he shook his head. "It's not just the money. We're in the country illegally. If we ask for help, the immigration people will find out and send us back to Mexico. There is no work there. We would starve."

Mary Beth was stunned. She had no idea of how to cut through the bureaucratic red tape, but she knew she had to do something.

"If you don't ask, your baby is going to die," she said harshly, and winced at her own brutality. She knew it was the only way to get through to this confused and frightened man.

The mother cried out in her anguish, and the father slumped and ran his hand across his face. "We don't know any doctors," he said hopelessly.

"I'll get you one," she answered. "Do you have a telephone?"

They didn't, and after a few more questions, she left and drove to the gas station on the corner to use the public phone. There was one number she could call and be certain that her plea would be answered.

"Dr. Warren's office. May I help you?" said the voice at the other end of the line.

"This is Mary Beth," she said crisply, certain that the receptionist would remember her. "I must speak to the doctor, it's an emergency."

The woman switched her without replying, and Mary Beth's whole body tingled when his familiar baritone voice responded. "Dr. Warren speaking."

She closed her eyes, and his handsome face appeared to torment her. "Flynn, this is Mary Beth." Her voice was low and sexy, although that was not what she'd intended.

There was a pause, then he answered, "Yes, Mary Beth?" He might have been talking to the parent of any patient.

Her disappointment left her breathless. Given a choice, she would rather he had growled at her than shown no emotion at all.

Quickly she told him about the sick child and the difficult situation the family was in. "The baby is having difficulty breathing, Flynn," she finished. "I'm afraid she's dangerously ill."

He's asked a few terse questions as she'd talked, and now he said, "Do the parents have a car?"

"They own an old truck, but it doesn't have a heater."

"Then you bring the mother and child to Scripps Memorial Hospital in your car, and tell the father to follow in the truck. The emergency entrance is at the back. I'll meet you there. Drive carefully and don't speed."

They arranged to leave Juanita with a neighbor, and half an hour later Flynn met them at the hospital as he'd promised. In spite of her anxiety over the baby, Mary Beth had been unable to suppress her excitement at the prospect of seeing Flynn again as she'd sped down the freeway.

Her heart pounded and her hands shook as she shepherded her charges into the emergency area, but he barely acknowledged her as she introduced the Messa family. "Bring the baby and come with me," he said to the parents. "Mrs. Warren can wait here or..." For the first time he turned and spoke to her directly. "Will you be leaving?"

He called her "Mrs. Warren" with no more warmth than if she'd been "Mrs. Smith," and his tone indicated that she was being dismissed. Was he now thinking of her as his *ex*-wife just when she'd gotten used to thinking of him as her husband again? The idea made her feel sick as she shook her head. "No, I'll stay. Will you please come and tell me how the child is when you know?"

She wondered if he understood that she was telling him she wanted to see him when he was free.

For just an instant his gaze met hers before he broke the contact. ''Yes,'' was all he said as he walked away.

For almost two hours Mary Beth's anxiety mounted. There was still a lingering concern for the child, of course, but she knew the little girl was getting the best possible medical care. The source of her apprehension now was Flynn's attitude.

He obviously meant exactly what he'd said that morning two weeks ago. Always before when they'd quarreled, he'd been the first to make a move toward reconciliation. This time he hadn't called or made any attempt to get in touch with her, and just now he'd treated her as if she were an acquaintance he didn't like very much.

Well, what had she expected? Had she honestly thought he'd go along indefinitely with her loving him one moment and rejecting him the next? How could he know what she felt for him if she didn't even know herself?

Except that she did know. She'd always loved Flynn Warren. He was her first date, her first kiss, her first infatuation and her only lover. In the three years when she'd thought she was free, she'd dated and she'd been kissed, but the dates had been mere distractions from her haunting loneliness, and the kisses only innocent socially acceptable thank-yous for her escorts.

But what about Flynn? He'd been faithful to her during those years, and she'd repaid him by rejecting him yet again. It was true he should have told her that he'd had the divorce petition set aside. She had a right to be angry, but it wasn't the end of the world. He'd done it because he loved her and wanted her to be his wife. Was that really so awful?

When had she lost sight of the most important truth of all? The fact that her newfound independence and freedom were but cold, barren ashes, without someone to love, someone to love her.

Mary Beth was sitting on a chair, thumbing sightlessly through a magazine, when Flynn finally appeared. She was strung so tightly that she heard and recognized his footsteps in the hall even before he came into the room. She stood as he walked toward her, but his expression told her nothing. It was the impatient look of a harried physician squeezing in time to report on the condition of his patient.

"Sorry it took so long," he said impersonally, "but we had to wait for test reports and X rays. The child has a viral pneumonia, but thanks to you I think we've gotten it in time. We're admitting her to the hospital, but I'm optimistic about her chance for recovery."

Relief flooded through Mary Beth. Thank God, the baby was going to be all right. "Oh, I'm so glad. I knew you'd make her well if anyone could."

He frowned. "I'm not God, Mary Beth, but neither am I Satan." His tone was abrasive. "I think it's about time you accepted the fact that I'm just an imperfect man and stop expecting me to perform miracles, then blaming me when I can't."

Her eyes widened with distress. "But I don't—"

"The parents will be staying for a while," he interrupted, cutting off her protest. "You can go on home. I'm sure the parents will keep you informed."

He was dismissing her—telling her to go home and stay out of his life, but she couldn't do that. Without him she had no future, only a past.

He started to turn away from her and leave. Without thinking, she reached out and clasped his arm. "Flynn, please, I want to talk to you."

He turned back to her, disengaging her hand in the process. "Why?" he asked harshly. "If you want to tell me you're filing for dissolution of our marriage, we really have nothing to say to each other. Have your lawyer call me and I'll give him the name of mine. They can handle it. I told you I wouldn't contest it."

Divorce. Her stomach lurched. Is that what he really wanted?

"I'm not going to file for dissolution." Her voice shook, and she took a deep breath. "I just want to talk to you."

He still showed no emotion as he looked at his watch. "All right, if you'll come to the office with me, we can talk there."

His office was just a few steps across the parking lot from the hospital, but she knew she couldn't say what she wanted to in that sterile setting. "I don't want to consult you, Flynn, I want to go to your house and have a personal conversation."

At last she got a reaction from him. He looked startled. "I don't think that's a good idea—"

"Are you going to make me beg?" She heard the heartbreak in her tone.

Apparently he did, too, because his shoulders slumped as he sighed. "No, of course not, if it's that important to you. You go ahead. Lars will let you in. I have a few things to finish up at the office, but it won't take long."

This time when he turned from her, he walked away and disappeared into the bowels of the hospital.

Mary Beth's nervousness and apprehension increased with each mile as she drove toward Flynn's home. What if he didn't want her anymore? Judging by his attitude this afternoon, that seemed to be a definite possibility.

By the time she stood in front of his locked courtyard gate and rang the bell, she was trembling with tension. She jumped when Lars's voice, seemingly from out of nowhere, spoke. "May I help you?"

Belatedly realizing that the lock was connected to a PA system, she answered, "It's Mary Beth, Lars. I'm meeting Flynn."

There was a pause before the gate swung open. Lars met her at the door and silently motioned her inside. His face was impassive, but she managed a weak smile. "It's nice to see you up and around. Did the burns do much damage to your leg?"

He shrugged as he led her into the living room. "Not much. Does the boss know you're here?" She heard the disapproval in his tone.

"Yes, he does," she said as she took off her coat and handed it to him. "I know you don't like me, but I promise you, I don't want to hurt him."

"You have a damn funny way of showin' it," he muttered. "Will you be stayin' for dinner?"

She had smelled the heavenly aroma of beef stewing in beer as soon as she'd stepped in. "I don't know. I'd like to if Flynn doesn't throw me out before you get around to serving it. Did he tell you what we quarreled about?"

Lars nodded curtly. "Yeah. I agree he was outa line doin' what he did about the divorce, but hell, you didn't have to knee him in the groin for it."

Her head jerked up. "I didn't!"

"Just a figure of speech," he growled, "and don't kid yourself, lady, you did. The doc's hurtin', and you got a lot to answer for."

He left her then and went to hang her coat in the closet, while she headed for the bathroom to freshen up. She was wearing a gray wool skirt and a soft pink cashmere sweater, and a touch of lipstick was all the makeup she needed. A few tendrils of hair had come loose from her French braid, but they softened the anxious lines of her face and she left them alone.

She'd just returned to the living room when she heard a key in the door and Flynn came in. He was met by Lars, who took his coat, then said, "Your missus is here and dinner's ready. Why don't you two eat now, then I can clean up the kitchen and get out of the way."

Flynn looked up as Mary Beth joined them. "Is that all right with you?" he asked.

"Fine," she answered, thinking that the act of eating a hot meal together might ease some of the tension between them.

She was wrong. The dinner was delicious, but she hardly tasted it. Flynn spoke only when necessary. He looked tired, and she knew that she was only adding to his burdens. But then, hadn't she always?

The meal was finally over when they both declined dessert and went into the living room. Lars had a fire going in the fireplace, and Mary Beth settled in one corner of the sofa while Flynn lowered himself to the stone hearth and sat facing her.

He'd taken off his suit coat, but was still wearing the dark trousers, a white oxford shirt and a maroon tie. She wished he'd at least remove the tie and unbutton his collar, but didn't dare suggest it. He looked stiff and forbidding.

After a few moments of silence she patted the cushion beside her and blurted, "Why don't you come over here where you can be more comfortable?"

"I doubt that I'd be more at ease over there," he said frostily. "What is it you want to talk to me about?"

He was resisting her every step of the way, and she knew she'd made a mistake by forcing this meeting. Closing her eyes, she took a deep breath and prayed for guidance.

"Flynn," she began carefully, "I'm sorry for the way I've behaved. It was just such a shock when you told me we were still married."

"I know that," he replied reasonably. "I've admitted that I was wrong to interfere with the divorce."

She shook her head. "No, that's not what I mean. We're both to blame for the things that have gone wrong between us. It's not so much that you were wrong, or I was wrong, as that fate threw us together in a difficult situation and then left us to muddle through without any guidelines."

"I suppose," he said dully. "You said that you haven't filed for dissolution, yet—"

"No, Flynn, I said I *wasn't going* to file. I don't want our marriage dissolved. I love you."

He looked up and frowned; it was not at all the reaction she'd dared to hope for. "I don't think there's much doubt about our love for each other." His tone was still cool. "But I'll never be able to give you what you want, or live up to your expectations."

"That's not true," she protested as she got up and went to kneel in front of him. She touched his knees, and they parted to allow her to move closer. "I know I've been quarrelsome and abrasive. I don't blame you for being disgusted with me, I'm disgusted with myself."

She moved her hands a few inches up his thighs and felt his muscles twitch. At least his body still reacted to her nearness, but she wasn't trying to seduce him. She wanted so much more than that.

He put his hands over hers, but whether to stop them or because he needed to touch her she didn't know.

"Don't apologize for maturing over the years—it's a natural part of growing up," he said. "You were a child when I married you, and I did you no favor by consummating that marriage."

She lowered her head, unwilling to let him see how badly his words had hurt her. "Do you wish you hadn't?"

He drew in his breath and moved his hands to cup her face, then lifted it so she had to look at him. "For your sake I wish I'd had the guts to send you away before it got to the point where I had to have you no matter what," he said softly. "But for me—" his thumbs brushed her cheeks "—I wouldn't give up the years we had together for anything, not even your peace of mind. You gave me everything I wanted or needed in a wife, and I'll always be grateful. I was the one who spoiled it, and this time I think I'm strong enough to set you free. To give you a chance to find someone younger, more compatible, who can allow you the independence you crave."

She put her arms around his waist and snuggled against his chest. It was like coming home. Every inch of him had been explored by her and was indelibly printed on her psyche. She couldn't lose him. It would be like being pulled apart and left to bleed to death.

"Flynn, I have one question. Please think about it and answer it truthfully. It's important, and nothing but the honest truth will do."

His arms stole around her, and he rubbed his cheek in her hair. "I'll try."

Now that she was faced with asking, she wasn't sure she wanted to know. What if he said . . .

She tried to keep her voice steady. "Do you really and truly want out of our marriage? I don't mean, do you think it would be better for me, or the right thing to do? I just have to know if you would prefer not to be married to me anymore.''

His arms tightened around her, and she could feel his heart pound under her ear. "That's a complicated question. It can't be answered with a yes or no...."

A stab of fear almost paralyzed her. Was he hedging in order not to hurt her feelings? Had she truly killed his love with her childish temper tantrums?

"It has to be answered that way," she said, and her voice shook. "That's the basic issue here. We're at a crossroads, and what we do now will set the course for the rest of our lives. We can no longer afford the luxury of sparing each other's feelings."

For a long moment he didn't answer, and her terror grew. Why hadn't she left well enough alone? She could have seduced him and made him feel guilty enough to take her back. What difference did it make? She was desperate enough to take him any way she could get him.

When he finally spoke, it wasn't with an answer to her question but an observation. "As long as you're my wife, I'll continue to be possessive. It's a part of my nature that I can't always control. Could you accept that and live with it?"

She nodded against his shirt. "Yes. I'd rebel because you'd need to be reminded that I'm an adult and can make my own decisions, but it would put a little spice in our lives."

For the first time, he relaxed somewhat and chuckled. "Sweetheart, I don't think I could survive much more spice."

Sweetheart! The endearment tugged at her heart. She was making progress.

His levity was short-lived, however because when he spoke again, his tone was serious. "Would you transfer to another school if I asked you to?"

This time she hesitated, but only briefly. "Yes, I would, because I know you fear for my safety, but I'd hope we could reach a compromise. I could get used to my own personal security officer if he were available for the other teachers, as well."

He relaxed even more and hugged her close. "My dear, sweet wife," he murmured as he slid his hand under her sweater. "You don't have to make compromises with me. There's not a chance in hell that I'd ever have been able to let you walk out of my life, no matter how noble I happened to be feeling. You *are* my life, darling. Don't you know that?"

His fingers found her breast and stroked it, sending shivers of delight to her very center. "The answer to your question is no," he said as he kissed the pounding pulse in her throat. "No, I don't want out of this marriage. Why do you think I went to so much trouble, and risked your wrath, to preserve it after you left?"

Mary Beth didn't know which was arousing her the most, the things he was saying or the things he was doing to her. They were being given a second chance to make their unorthodox marriage work, and this time she wasn't going to mess up.

Flynn would banish the nightmare and free her to dream again of love.

*   *   *   *   *

COMING NEXT MONTH

#694 ETHAN—Diana Palmer—A Diamond Jubilee Title!
Don't miss *Ethan*—he's one Long, Tall Texan who'll have your heart roped and tied!

#695 GIVEAWAY GIRL—Val Whisenand
Private investigator Mike Dixon never meant to fall in love with Amy Alexander. How could he possibly tell her the painful truth about her mysterious past?

#696 JAKE'S CHILD—Lindsay Longford
The moment Jake Donnelly arrived with a bedraggled child, Sarah Jane Simpson felt a strange sense of foreboding. Could the little boy be her long-lost son?

#697 DEARLY BELOVED—Jane Bierce
Rebecca Hobbs thought a visit to her sleepy southern hometown would be restful. But handsome minister Frank Andrews had her heart working overtime!

#698 HONEYMOON HIDEAWAY—Linda Varner
Divorce lawyer Sam Knight was convinced that true love was a myth. But Libby Turner, a honeymoon hideaway manager, was set to prove him wrong with one kiss as evidence....

#699 NO HORSING AROUND—Stella Bagwell
Jacqui Prescott was determined to show cynical Spencer Matlock she was a capable jockey. But then she found herself suddenly longing to come in first in the sexy trainer's heart!

AVAILABLE THIS MONTH:

#688 FATHER CHRISTMAS
Mary Blayney

#689 DREAM AGAIN OF LOVE
Phyllis Halldorson

#690 MAKE ROOM FOR NANNY
Carol Grace

#691 MAKESHIFT MARRIAGE
Janet Franklin

#692 TEN DAYS IN PARADISE
Karen Leabo

#693 SWEET ADELINE
Sharon De Vita

✦ *Silhouette Romances*®

DIAMOND JUBILEE
CELEBRATION!

It's Silhouette Books' tenth anniversary, and what better way to celebrate than to toast *you*, our readers, for making it all possible. Each month in 1990, we'll present you with a DIAMOND JUBILEE Silhouette Romance written by an all-time favorite author!

Welcome the new year with *Ethan*—a LONG, TALL TEXANS book by Diana Palmer. February brings Brittany Young's *The Ambassador's Daughter*. Look for *Never on Sundae* by Rita Rainville in March, and in April you'll find *Harvey's Missing* by Peggy Webb. Victoria Glenn, Lucy Gordon, Annette Broadrick, Dixie Browning and many more have special gifts of love waiting for you with their DIAMOND JUBILEE Romances.

Be sure to look for the distinctive DIAMOND JUBILEE emblem, and share in Silhouette's celebration. Saying thanks has never been so romantic. . . .

**Diana Palmer brings you an Award of Excellence
title ... and the first Silhouette Romance DIAMOND
JUBILEE book.**

ETHAN
by Diana Palmer

This month, Diana Palmer continues her bestselling
LONG, TALL TEXANS series with *Ethan*—the story
of a rugged rancher who refuses to get roped and tied
by Arabella Craig, the one woman he can't resist.

The Award of Excellence is given to one
specially selected title per month. Spend
January with *Ethan* #694 ... a special
DIAMOND JUBILEE title ... only in
Silhouette Romance.

Ethan-1

SILHOUETTE DESIRE™
presents
AUNT EUGENIA'S TREASURES
by CELESTE HAMILTON

Liz, Cassandra and Maggie are the honored recipients of Aunt Eugenia's heirloom jewels...but Eugenia knows the real prizes are the young women themselves. Read about Aunt Eugenia's quest to find them everlasting love. Each book shines on its own, but together, they're priceless!

Available in December:
THE DIAMOND'S SPARKLE (SD #537)

Altruistic Liz Patterson wants nothing to do with Nathan Hollister, but as the fast-lane PR man tells Liz, love is something he's willing to take *very* slowly.

Available in February:
RUBY FIRE (SD #549)

Impulsive Cassandra Martin returns from her travels... ready to rekindle the flame with the man she never forgot, Daniel O'Grady.

Available in April:
THE HIDDEN PEARL (SD #561)

Cautious Maggie O'Grady comes out of her shell...and glows in the precious warmth of love when brazen Jonah Pendleton moves in next door.

Wonderful, luxurious gifts can be yours with proofs-of-purchase from any specially marked ''Indulge A Little'' Harlequin or Silhouette book with the Offer Certificate properly completed, plus a check or money order (do not send cash) to cover postage and handling payable to Harlequin/Silhouette ''Indulge A Little, Give A Lot'' Offer. We will send you the specified gift.

Mail-in-Offer

Item	OFFER CERTIFICATE			
	A Collector s Doll	B Soaps in a Basket	C Potpourri Sachet	D Scented Hangers
# of Proofs-of -Purchase	18	12	6	4
Postage & Handling	$3.25	$2.75	$2.25	$2.00
Check One				

Name _____

Address _____ Apt # _____

City _____ State _____ Zip _____

ONE PROOF OF PURCHASE

To collect your free gift by mail you must include the necessary number of proofs-of-purchase plus postage and handling with offer certificate

SR-3

Harlequin®/Silhouette®

Mail this certificate, designated number of proofs-of-purchase and check or money order for postage and handling to·

INDULGE A LITTLE
P.O. Box 9055
Buffalo, N.Y. 14269-9055